BLUE
RAVEN

LANE

Fulton Books, Inc.
Meadville, PA

Published by Fulton Books 2021

ISBN 978-1-64952-742-4 (paperback)
ISBN 978-1-64952-744-8 (digital)

Printed in the United States of America

I dedicate this book to Alexandria. A person, a place an important thing in my heart, always whether near or far. Don't ever forget that because I have not.

I Love you with my whole heart.

CONTENTS

INTRODUCTION

Although it is a fictitious book art imitating life, in some circles, it is life imitating art unfortunately. This book was written to shed light on some of the perils that young women and young men have endured—from abuse at home or from someone you think you love or even one you think you can look up to. Do not be gaslighted. Those that are truly weak have a propensity to do this. You need to know it isn't a must to endure certain things in life. If you see something, say something so someone can do something. A stop needs to come to it. If it is you, do not let it be all in vain and know there is a light at the end of the tunnel. This book is to let you know that you are strong and that you are loved and to believe in yourself—to understand that your decisions in life are your decisions alone, even if and when you make mistakes. They are decisions that you will grow and learn from. Do realize that no one shall have dominion over you except for your Lord and Savior.

Do not let yourself take abuse, and hopefully identify those that want to subject you or somebody you know to it. Whatever you decide to do, do it with a purpose and don't let it define you but let it be a means to an end. For the love of each other, don't be hateful nor cruel, for we never know what someone is living through. This life is too short, not guaranteed to anyone. Thus whoever you love, that is your choice. Your heart has guided you there.

With this being said, perhaps one day, you can pay it forward. "Let all things be done in love" (Corinthians 16:14).

INVIDIOUS ACT

The day

The sun had just barely risen, for there was still a dewy mist in the air. He walked up to find her lying in an industrial alleyway on broken glass, nude from the waist down, insentient.

There was a trace of a slight milky but clear liquid on her inner thigh. He panned over her entire body with his eyes then stooped down to pick her up.

He carried Raven back to the house and to her sister Meaghan he was married to. He then placed Raven's limp body down on the couch and said, "Well, I found her." Cuts, scrapes, and bruises were mapping out her backside ass area and partial legs. Her sister said, "Looks as if she's been raped!"

Mark, her brother-in-law, then said, "Well, I guess I will call 9-1-1." So authorities were then contacted. At this point, she was fully awake with no absolute recollection of the night before or how she even got back to the house. She just knew she last left jumping in the back of a friend's pickup.

Raven was undertaking a barrage of questioning as nothing was ringing a bell, feeling as if the walls were closing in on her and much loss with a sense of reality, not knowing whether coming or going from such a nefarious occurrence sent her on a downward spiral of sexual depravity of attempting suicide, of course, but failing with her futile attempt. Living in Upstate New York was a blah life Raven felt, which had already brought about a depressed state of mind! This indeed was a strong catalyst in causing her to have a weak state of just being her, sometimes wishing she would have met her demise due to

9

infanticide! Although a very pretty fresh face, a full figure, very natural, with a mixture of ethnicities, she was still looked upon as a mutt.

She was just letting worthlessness, pity, and self-loathing get the best of her—to the point of being so unhinged to attempt suicide again and not speaking for about a month to a month and a half to friends and family upon their visits to her ward. Yes, a ward—just rocking back and forth in a chair.

She was locked away in a place for the "crazies," where feces and urine were spread upon the walls and the magnificent stench taking one under—such a deplorable setting in an old building with rusted wrought iron gates and unkept grounds. It was astonishing how that place was even allowed to be opened—not to mention the screamers. Screamers were those so gone. They say they just sit in any open area, screaming then mumbling some strange shit to themselves. Her family did come to take a firmer grasp at the reality of the situation to get her into what was an adequate facility. A cousin of hers came visiting there, and there was one of the patients in the hallway literally trying to stick his hand up to his own ass. How one would even manage such a feat is mind-blowing. Her family really needed to get her into a more pleasant living environment for one so she did not completely crack. They pulled out all resources together they could come up with, and a big chunk of it came from her cousin in conjunction with the government's help, and it worked.

Thus, as times progressed, in now a better facility, the Cirtaihc Institute with tall bleached-white columns on the outside, a peach beige-color structure, manicured grounds, which looked like a decked-out mansion, she began to open up and get a sense of normalcy, even though she was housed with a schizophrenic thrash metalhead roommate named Tara, who was administered a high dose of Thorazine, washed-out overly processed bleached hair, dark circles under her eyes, but not so skinny with a pancake ass with what looked like individual slashes on her neck. Some looked rather fresh. On her wall above her bed, she wrote in a marker over a metal poster, "I'm the sister of Satan."

Raven just looked then said, "Okay, I am Raven." Tara said nothing then rolled her eyes to the back of her head until they turned white. The nurse Harbour came in, wearing pure white scrubs, pristine white shoes, hair pulled back so tightly Raven thought her eyes were to pop out, and she said, "Welcome, Ms. Raven Foslear. Dear, you have nothing to worry about. She's harmless. Her medicine makes her eyes do that. Oh, and she's not the sister of Satan."

Raven just shrugged her shoulders and said, "No biggie. My mother suffers from schizophrenia with a touch of bipolar disorder, my family has been saying for years. Guess it could be an underlying reason why I am here and threatened to kill myself, who knows really."

Nurse Harbour said, "Oh dear, I am aware we have been briefed on your situation. Rest assure we are going to take good care of you. Also, here are some blue slippers for you. We know your favorite color is blue, and we try to give each patient something good that they can connect with. Yours are these slippers since, in your last dwelling, one of the patients got a hold of your slippers and shit in them." As she said, "Shit in them," she leaned in closer with her hand on Raven's shoulder, speaking it lowly, softly, almost with a whisper.

Then another girl named Michelle came in and grabbed her hand, saying, "Hi, Raven, I'm Michelle. Let me show you around." She was the heavyset. She was very pretty with thin fine features, the girl with a chubby face, and always wore her hair in two ponytails, silky long and dark, that liked to skip through the halls in the day so happily. Raven felt like she was someone she could actually befriend and have more common ground with.

"This nuthouse is very clean," Raven said. Michelle laughed and said, "It's not a nuthouse, silly. It's our house, for now, to hold us and watch over us and keep us safe and others safe from us, if you know what I mean."

Raven admittedly said, "Michelle, I am here because I was going to try to kill myself from a rape that I have no recollection of. Accept from what I have been told, which is killing me because I feel as if I should remember details you know, and my brother, well, my sister's husband, would molest me repeatedly. I haven't hurt anyone nor have tried. I just really spoke my thoughts out loud, and apparently, it caused an uproar hence ending up," then looked around with her hands up.

Michelle said, "First off, I am glad you are talking. I heard you were mute." Raven's eyes got really small as she squinted at Michelle. "I feel your pain, Raven. Look at this," Michelle said. Then she lifted up the sleeves of her hospital pants and the sleeves of her shirt and showed Raven all these scars, these slash marks—kind of looked like the ones that Tara, her roommate, had on her neck. Michelle then said, "They're not the same as Tara's. She says some creature comes to her at night and makes her do that. Since they always look fresh, the nurses and staff had to start restraining her to her bed at night. Mine, scoffing. Well, my scars, they are from my very own mother that would hold me down, shoot me up with heroin, then allow multiple men to have sex with me. She would record it and would sell the footage. Then she would remind me to stay quiet about it with a slash either here or down here, totaling up to thirteen on my upper limbs and nine on my lower," pointing to her wrists and arm areas and ankles and top of her feet.

Raven was just completely stoic at that point and said to herself, "Maybe all monsters are human."

"Apparently, my dear mother said I had been taken and put on this entire Broadway production of sorts. Had everyone feeling sorry for her. Don't worry though, Raven, she's gone and will not hurt me anymore when I do get out."

"Gone?" Raven said.

Michelle said, "Mmm, hmm, she's gone. I killed the bitch, my very own mother. As far as my dad, in case you are wondering, my cunt of a mother drove him away into the arms of a man. Could have helped in making her even more fucking crazy who knows."

There is always something bigger than you and what your troubles may be, Raven thought. Michelle continued on to say, "Actually, there was a point where I blocked these memories, I guess to protect my own well-being doc says. Perhaps waiting until a moment where I truly felt safe. Anyway, let's just stay in the moment of now."

Raven just looked downward, squinting her eyes some, then shook it off as Michelle finished showing Raven the common areas of a nice large facility where she said, "This one side is just for us young girls and young women, and the other side through a thick big steel door was for the boys or young men. Also, this is our dining hall, and we get to watch movies and different programming and eat popcorn and snacks, but we have to take our meds. This is our crafting room. The large area through the other doors is our indoor gym with an indoor pool. Come see. We also have a pool outside enclosed within large walls both us girls and the boys on the other side are able to use it though."

Raven just looked around, saying, "Wow, this is like something out of a movie. This place is fucking amazing."

As Michelle began skipping down the hallway like an almost full-grown kid, she then said, "Yes, it is, and I get to live here two more years and out when I am twenty-one." Being there has helped Michelle come to terms with her life as she knew it to previously be and to come to terms with being a motherless child heading for womanhood. "Doctor Mohibi is really good, Raven. She's a female and patient and kind. She has truly helped me a lot and will help you too. We meet with her in group sessions twice a week for an hour and then one-on-ones once a week for an hour."

Raven actually began to enjoy her stay there at the Cirtaihc Facility Institution as she was heading to her second one-on-one with Doctor Mohibi, a very pretty doctor, Indian or Middle Eastern but spoke like she had pop rocks in her mouth, you know the candy. So sometimes, it was hard for Raven to fully understand her, but she managed. She would always start off her sessions by saying namaste then coming closer and putting her fingers on your temples, lightly pressing then rubbing them softly. This indeed was some sort of calming mechanism, and she was good.

Now comes the day of Raven to be released to go home to a disheveled hovel of a dwelling that they made the most of to be with her siblings and her fucked mother. She felt as if she had a duty to her mother to watch over her in a sense. She wasn't going back to stay with her damn sister and that piece-of-shit man she calls a husband. There was only less than a year for her until she was technically an adult anyway. Her release was delayed momentarily because Tara tried to jump the wall outside by the pool and either escape or try to off herself—quite possibly an attempt to do the latter of the two. Michelle came running up and said, "Hey, Raven, Tara is banged up pretty bad. That's why they won't let you leave yet, being you two are, well, were roommates and all. They said she was trying to escape. I think she was trying to, you know." Then she made the motion of a knife slitting across her throat, the symbolization of Tara trying to slit her own throat off herself die.

Raven just took a deep breath, slowly exhaling. Shaking her head, she did not say a word. She just began to think of starting a new and to find herself her purpose and blossom into the young lady she needed to become. Again, she could not go back to the living situation at her older sister and that brother-in-law's house, given the fact that she also went through a brief period of molestation from him. She saw vivid visions of Mark watching her in the shower on a stool placed under the window, also hiding in her bedroom from inside her closet watching her and masturbating to the point where he would sneak out in the main part of the room and fondle her breasts and vaginal area with even getting in a lick from time to time on her. One night, he and her sister were out and came back in late. Meaghan was really drunk and passed out that Mark had to carry her inside, putting her in the bed. That was the night he sneaked into her room, fully naked, saying, "Raven, Raven, you awake?"

She didn't answer, thinking her silence this time might make him go away. Well, that did not work in her favor because he then started rubbing his nasty self all over her. She couldn't even sleep fully dressed in her bed because he held a plastic bag over her head one time, threatening her that she better sleep nude or damn near close to it. He then said to Raven, "If you say anything to your sister, I will just deny it profusely and have you thrown out and you and your sister beaten to a bloody mess, you got me?" She nodded her head yes while the plastic bag was still wrapped around it. He finally took it off, and she gasped for air like it was the first time she had ever breathed in her life. He then put it back on, making her have forcible sex with him. This act or acts, if you will, happened repeatedly. It was like living on the same night over and over and over again. It's like he started to get greedy just knowing he could do what he wanted when he wanted to Raven. There was even a night when he entered her room and was really high. He told her to lie there silent and still as he placed some blow on her stomach and snorted it off. Poor Raven. How was she even to get out of this hell?

Raven stayed silent and let him just have his way with her until he was done and removed himself. She was all cried out at that point. Eventually, she told another sister who swore with every fucking bone in her body that she would be sworn to secrecy, that she would stay hush. Unfortunately, it didn't fucking ever work out that way. Learning later that people were blatantly cold and self-serving, she had to escape and get away fending for herself. This was to take a little more time though because she didn't quite hit her eighteen-year mark yet. If only she was to stay at Cirtaihc Institute until that time, unfortunately not. There wasn't enough money to fund it from her family, especially the government—most likely, a problem that the government deemed not so much of a problem. It was on the lower end of the scale for them.

Therefore, she did her best to wait patiently for that day to arrive. So impatient she was, but who would not be? Raven believed she had to get everything she needed to help her come to terms with the affliction. There was just a thing that she could not put her finger on. Not wanting this to affect her later on, she thought she did not want to get out and be so impetuous that would not be of any benefit to her well-being at all. She thought of Michelle and how she seemed so strong and ready for the world. "How does she keep it together, so composed and aware but happy?" It was an admiring trait Michelle had, and Raven adored that and respected it. Raven was strong herself and resilient. She just was not aware of how much. She blamed herself too much in her therapy session with Dr. Mohibi, where the doctor finally told her, "You have got to stop blaming yourself. It is not your fault. The person at fault is a degenerate that preys on young women such as yourself. There is a sickness within him."

It was hard at times to really block out the horrible memories from what Mark would do to her repeatedly, although she tried and silently wished him dead. "Why do I have these horrific scenes of what he did to me play back in my mind over and over, and then I have no recollection of my actual rape?" She remembered asking the doctor this specific question.

Doctor Mohibi said, "This is part of the trauma you have suffered and are still suffering from. Maybe there is a part of you that thinks he is truly responsible for your rape or knows of the person behind it and is perhaps protecting them. This could all be connected because usually, in cases like this, it is. In time, it shall reveal, or maybe it'll be too hurtful that you keep it locked away forever as a coping mechanism, a way of just protecting yourself, dear. The human mind is a very interesting thing. Very quirky but very complex, the mind is a set of thinking faculties, like our judgment, consciousness, imagination, and memory. I think it is safe to say that you are experiencing dissociative amnesia, which was brought on by fugue. This is why you do not recall the events of that night or what led up to it. You just had to take flight in your case, jumping on the back of a neighbor guy friend's truck, probably trying to escape your brother-in-law, which sounds like the most obvious to me."

Raven, all bright-eyed, just staring like a dear caught in headlights, just swallowed hard. She then said, "My god, I didn't think of it like that."

Doctor Mohibi said, "How and why would you? You were still a child when this started taking place, and now you're not much short of being a young woman. Do not blame yourself as most often victims like to do. You will get through this, Raven. You are still an attractive young girl and resilient. Even when you are released, I'd like you to feel free to contact me at your discretion, of course."

Such bad memories of her sister's house, so when it came to when she was finally released, she did not go back over there. She went back home with her schizo mom, the lesser of the two evils. Then at that ripe age she was waiting for, she bolted into New York City to be exact. Raven said, "I need to find me and experience real love and real life if there is somewhere for me." She explored the bright lights of the big city, the noise, the "forget about it" people she passed, just the overall ambiance of it all. Oh, how she thought this to be grand, an epic adventure in different ways that would maybe help her find herself.

Will and can things get better when trying to escape the darkness and getting away from what you think is your hell? One only knows.

Do things get worse before they get better?

CHAPTER 1

EVELYN SEXISODE

A sexisode is an episode of sexual pleasure, willing participants, of course. It can make for a quite fulfilling moment or moments in time with someone that feels the same about you. Let's begin an episodic sexisode adventure.

Stepping into young womanhood, she felt a strong desire to get out of the box. She needed something more that she knew was not readily available in the mundane existence she knew. Feeling better, she realized life still had a chance to offer her something appeasing. "Is that all of me? Was the best taken from me?" There was an existential existence, and she was bound to find it. She wanted to experience the good within all the bad and felt it possible. She opted for New York City. "What could be better, right?"

Raven arrived in New York City after hopping on train after train, finally embarking into Times Square. She stumbled upon a club. She knew she had to get into something to start earning some money and quick. She encountered men dressed as women fighting on the street corner over high heels. *Strange, welcome to New York,* she thought. There were several spots she walked past with guys outside, trying to urge her to come in. Finally, she stumbled on a quaint stinky and stifling little spot where she got hired and danced in a cage upstairs, making more money than any after school job paid her previously. Also, she found another spot for sexual peeping and a wide stage of her own to dance her heart out, captivating all who viewed.

There, Raven met a sizzling hot Latin chick named Evelyn, who was so intriguingly sexy, who became her first girl-on-girl sexual experience, deliciously exciting, with soft, supple olive skin, voluptuously large tits, lips ever so saying come kiss me. They soon ended up being roommates with moving into Queens, Corona, Queens to be exact.

Evelyn would taunt and tease so much that she could feel her pussy pulsating, and it had never even been touched by her. Time lapsed, and they would go to different nightclub outings and party and dance the night away. Then one evening, another friend of Evelyn was out and about. She approached them, and they started dancing, their bodies flowing with the music in sync. Then they kissed ever so passionately, each other's tongue swirling around in the other's mouth and all over their lips. Must say it was a gorgeous sight to behold, really wanting to partake in but exerting much control. She was always one for a subtle presentation of the sort, drawing her in, closer and closer. Finally, when they got back into Queens from the nightclub, they talked in the room for an hour. Then she kissed Raven, pushing her back on the bed, removing her clothing, kissing, and licking every inch of her tight body. Then placed her soft, hot mouth and lips on her pussy, tasting with every lick and kissing her clitoris while placing fingers inside her—sucking and licking her pussy in its whole. She exploded so intensely, squirting all in her mouth.

Completely embarrassed, feeling shameful, she got up and ran to the bathroom, barricading herself up against the door for about a good hour. Evelyn proceeded to knock and knock on the door. She remained stoic there but going through a myriad of emotion within—not to mention, her clitoris ever still swollen and her pussy pulsating from her touch, her lick, the softness of her lips, and the steam of her mouth. So then she finally answered her, saying, "Yes."

She said, "Are you okay? You've been in the bathroom for a minute!"

She responded, "I know. I'll be coming out soon." From the sound of it, it seemed like she already did.

Suffice it to it was a moment within the actual moments that she experienced within that sexisode of erotically wet, hot passion and desire that actually was thought to be mythological.

Then she replied, "I believe you already have!" followed by a chuckle!

Thus, as months passed, Raven and Evelyn moved in together. There was so much passion between the two women fueled from the lust that every waking hour it was an uncontrollable urge to devour each other. Of course, Evelyn was taking the reins and controlling all aspects of this dynamic between them. Evelyn was well seasoned in doing so. As time went, their love for each other blossomed quickly and intensely. Then one night, Raven was home alone. Her phone rang. She looked and shook her head. *Those two dos hombres gay.*

When you like, you like.

CHAPTER 2

DOS HOMBRES

"Those two dos hombres gay," Evelyn would call them often. Mario and Eric were so cute. What do you do? One friend of hers named Mario, and the other friend named Eric. There was indeed something about these two that Raven could not put her finger on. Evelyn did. Indeed, though, somehow, she knew. Mario used to be a male stripper until a close friend of his was shot. The story went as such. He was a close friend of his, named Carlos, who danced together at The Midnight Room down in the village. They would go to a nearby swinger's bar afterward every other night or so. There were couples that would flock these bars, looking to pick up men. They would use their wives as the bate to interest the men and sometimes offer money for them to fuck their wives while they watched—probably joining in at some point.

In any event, Mario and his friend were out and about when approached by a man with his wife wanting to swing. Carlos obliged the couple while Mario was not so interested. Carlos later left with the couple and was actually seeing them on quite a few different occasions. Unfortunately, one night, when Carlos went to meet up with the couple, the husband was dumb high, most likely hallucinating, shooting Carlos in the chest and later, saying it was because he had gotten to forcefully aggressive with his wife during sex, and he didn't like it. This was indeed a bunch of bullshit because Carlos was indeed homosexual and would never force himself on a woman. The story didn't come out for a while, even though Carlos was gone for three months. Mario would constantly contact him, and he didn't get any response. Mario just began to believe that Carlos ran off with someone else he met since he was a bit of a philanderer. When the news finally broke that Carlos was found and the cause of death was a bullet to the chest, Mario knew that was a sign to get out of the circuit and start new.

It weighed heavily on Mario because although Carlos was his friend, he crushed on him hard secretly. Mario even tried to just date women, but his full interest was never really there. He became close with Evelyn, which in turn opened the door to Raven, thinking that perhaps something could come of them. He didn't fully factor into the equation that Eric, his other close friend, was very sweet to him. It was something that she and Evelyn discussed, although Raven wasn't too convinced. Therefore, she decided to do an experiment by inviting them over. Absolutely, they both came over to just have a cool, relaxing time with Raven, which quickly turned into Mario kissing her then Eric kissing her, and they both wanted her, wanting to indulge in a moment of lustful sex three-way.

Raven stopped for a minute and said, "Okay! If you both wish to get some of the pleasures I have, I want you two to kiss each other and mean it. Let's do it now, boys." They stopped for a minute, eyes widening in amazement staring at one another. Then they turned and looked at her, pulling each other in to proceed with her command. As passionately and beautiful it was to see the two of them kiss, it was at the same time very shocking. Raven refused to go any further with this three-way. They were very respectful to her when she abruptly changed her mind. So she said, "Hey, why don't we hop on the train, take it into the city, and dance the night away?"

In the club, she was now the center of attention, dancing bodies throbbing and pulsating on the floor, men and women both desiring her so. Raven, warding off all advances, just danced and played with Mario and Eric, who were the envy of all who saw. She had to say to herself, "Damn it, Evelyn, you had an idea, and I was clueless but curious. Oh well, at this point, who cares? All is fair in love." That night brought on a promising love affair of Mario and Eric that made Raven smile. After all, they're her friends, first and foremost.

What was she really trying to see to prove to her inner voice she's been fighting against somewhere there lay the bitterroot.

Write a letter to that little girl or boy.

CHAPTER 3

THE ROOT

She was whaling and screaming in her sleep from a deep-rooted fear of some sort. These nightmares occurred on. *Constant*. They were so visceral and so surreal she started to question her own sanity. She soon realized that they stemmed from an ordeal she kept hidden away in her mind, a sort of dissociative amnesia to protect herself. When about fifteen, she dealt with molestation by her brother-in-law, who would creep in her room at night, hide in her closet, also position himself on a stool outside the bathroom window to watch as she undressed and showered and got out. This went on for months until she was seventeen in age, playing all the disgustingness back in her head. She became increasingly disturbed from it, rebelling and facing him to forewarn him of her knowledge of him creeping in, touching her with his hands and mouth as she slept, etcetera. She told him emphatically so that she's to tell her sister. His response was "If you do, she won't believe you, and I will beat her and you beyond recognition." Coming full circle to her rape and being left in an alley and he the only one coming to the rescue that found her nearly lifeless body. He was most definitely the culprit of this nefariousness. She would block the memory out for some time to come. Storing it in her subconscious to protect herself, kind of a subconscious block. These things are hard because if not dealt with accordingly, it can cause an uncomfortable sense in life especially when wanting and attempting something new. This she will soon to learn but after a series of unfortunate events. There's no constant father figure in her life, and her mother, she was just not really there, let's say. She cared when it was convenient, and when it was inconvenient, well, you get the idea. Then we have the sexual assault, molestation, rape, and threat of suicide. These were all a prelude to a lack of her self-worth, leading to the first step in low self-esteem. Low self-esteem is not something you are born with. It is developed depending on your environment, just a bottomless pit of never feeling quite good enough. Her soul opened to the demon of self-doubt. This all led to her allowing for domestic abuse, opening the door to further debauchery. Yes, debauchery at its finest—starting with the band.

Only for musical ears.

CHAPTER 4

THE BAND

Broken, lost, and feeling forgotten, now what? So she danced in the circuit of New York midtown area, coming across so many walks of life and a music group of members so diabolical and nefarious, not even worthy of names. She was dating one for a couple of years, especially if you're to call it that until he tied her up in a room and allowed his brother to enter then enter her unwillingly if you will, penetrating her so deep and hard feeling as if her spine was ripping out.

Completely unapologetic this band of misfits is, for sure, a chauvinistic bunch of misogynistic women abusers. What could she do though? No one would believe that is why so many get away with demeaning things as such. Niggas had niggas on standby if someone was to act out or deny them their desires and such. Also, they made sure girls were passed around like ragdolls. They loved to call them groupies and such. She stayed for a while, going from here to there when he wanted her, which was all she knew. There was indeed some type of hold he had on her that she was oblivious to, especially when he sat in front of the piano, played it, and began to sing—placed her under a spell. Something within the music made her feel as if she was on a level of something special, something other. Then he would threaten her into bringing various girls over to use as playthings, forcing them to go down on each other and so on and so forth. There was a sense of power that he got from demeaning her and demeaning any woman. When one challenged him and tried to emasculate his "manhood," he sexually assaulted her and burning her over 60 percent of her body all the way down through to the muscle. She blacked out from the excruciating pain, if not dying from. Then he wrapped her body up after pouring a fifth of vodka down her throat, then drove over to the Westside highway area, and left her body by water. Raven dared not say a thing against anything he put out that was negative. She saw and listened to other rooms too so much, so much torture and pain. Although that was the worst, leaving an innocent young woman's body wrapped after burned over half her body and thrown out. This was part of the catalyst to the in-between.

Abusers wear many faces.

CHAPTER 5

THE IN-BETWEEN

In between back and forth, up and down, she danced and danced from one main club to the next. There was constant drugging to remove her thoughts and vicious memories, setting herself up for what always was dismay. She'd visited various underground sex clubs of S-M, sometimes allowing herself to be spanked raw, thinking that this will mitigate any memories of a sort she felt that were negative. This was her pastime, her escape, her refuge from the egregious actions that had been bestowed upon her—acid tab after acid tab, a plethora of drugs from cocaine on, partying with greasy seedy wise guys that were gentle souls, nonetheless. To her, this was a kind of respite that was so needed. Or did something dark take over her unknowingly? Time would tell. Raven enjoyed going to what they call drag clubs as well, going and watching the "trannies," very flamboyant men who dressed as women and usually were not afraid to let you know. They'd go full throttle, dressing to the nines and all glammed-up lip-synching. It was quite a sight for sore eyes, at least to Raven. Raven would attend the different shows with a friend Gia. Most of the trannies anyway despised Raven and Gia and referenced them as "fish," meaning authentic lady parts on them. "Oh, here comes the fish!" or "The fish jumped out the river!" etc. Raven and Gia would find it to be quite comical. So they would sit and watch the shows like everyone else who entered the venue and rather enjoyed them. This is how she initially met Niki and Britany.

CHAPTER 6

NIKI AND BRITANY

Raven called Niki and Britany the darlings of the dance world—two quintessential beauties that came to be best friends and good friends with Raven. They were very interestingly funny, kind, sweet, and sexy. All you wanted to do was be yourself around them and be around them. Being in their presence was something that Raven enjoyed, just loving being around these two—all so young and spirited and very receptive to all. This was the only time Raven slept with more than one girl at a time. This was something that just came naturally to the three of them—a beautiful triangle of soft, supple breasts, lips, and skin. The three of them frequented Central Park to just reflect on life and speak of current events. When they hit the club circuit, it would be these three that would turn the nightclub upside down. There were lots of eyes staring with lust, jealousy, and hatred. There was a night when the three of them were supposed to go all out together, and Raven was too busy, still interacting in the tranny world with her friend Gia. In any event, Niki and Britany still went out to their favorite spot to dance and meet some guys from a previous outing that somehow made their way back to Niki and Britany's apartment on the upper west side.

Later that evening, Raven took a taxi up to their apartment, knowing they would be there because, at that time, it was almost 3:00 a.m. She basically would just walk up and in since she would be there often to walk the cutest little Yorkshire terrier named Uma. For she was something always happy bouncing and jumping like she had springs for legs, yet she was a Yorkie, not a Jack Russel as one would think. It was such a delightful dog to be around, just like her mom's with a pretty lavender bow on her collar. Raven proceeded up the stairs to let herself in. For some reason, the door wouldn't budge. Uma didn't bark like she normally did, especially as Raven approached the door.

"Hmm, that's a bit odd," Raven said to herself, but odder that the door was not budging but unlocked. Raven pushed against the door and pushed, calling out for Niki and Britany then calling for Uma—nothing but utter silence. She used her body to finally get the door open enough to slide in. It was dark from what she could see, except for a swinging light in the bathroom. As she went to slip in through the crack of the door, she lost her footing and fell over because the floor was all slick and wet. She knew it wasn't from Uma because of one thing, she did not mess in the house no matter what. She went to rise and wiped her hands on her pants and looked as the light flickered, somehow showing the silhouette of Britany's body lying on the floor bleeding out from her neck and multiple stab wounds on other parts of her body, even her face.

Raven went to scream but stifled it with her hands, not even caring about the residual blood on her hands. She started to approach the bathroom where the light was flickering and felt as if her feet, as she took each step, was like swimming. And she saw Niki lying in the tub with a sash from a robe around her neck and stab wounds in her breasts. She contacted the police and explained to them there has been a double homicide. She gave them the address but not her name. She was petrified. There was a plethora of blood all in the tub, and when she turned the lights on, the blood turned into a lake before her. Niki's eyes were open, open wide, but she was dead. She headed to the window where the fire escape was, noticing it had been left open, which faced the back of the building, the quiet side. She looked then looked closer again and saw Uma out there tied up to the railing. Raven ran to her, calling her name as she started to cry. Uma was still completely stoic and slowly looked up at Raven, her lavender bow looking burgundy. It was saturated with the blood of her mothers. Raven untied Uma and removed her bow, feeling parts of her fur also wet with blood and mixed with the spillage of bathwater.

She held Uma and cried as Uma also cried like dogs do in solemn moments. How can this be? Why her darlings, her loves? They were just that and more in a much deeper way than just sex. Raven loved them so much, and they her. This was another major pivotal moment in her life.

Soon the police came in, an entire force it seemed like. Guns were drawn and everything to find Raven tucked away in the corner, holding Uma, weeping profusely. She and Uma were escorted out of the building by Detective Alyna and her partner, Detective O' Hern. Once again, she was under the spotlight of a barrage of questioning from another damn nefarious occurrence. She began to yell, "I don't know anything else!" Raven explained to them how she was last told that they were at an underground nightclub in the Meatpacking District called The Tunnel. She gave them info on Niki's mother, who was back home in Boston, where Niki was originally from. Britany didn't have any family in New York that didn't disown her for dancing and her open adoration for women.

Raven had to turn Uma over for some type of weird testing, and detectives were saying forensics would work with animal control to make sure she didn't consume any of Niki or Britany's flesh or something like that. It seemed that it is what is said that animals do when they are trapped inside with the owner(s), and they die. "She was tied to the railing on the fire escape, so that would be virtually impossible," Raven said to the detective. Raven was then escorted home and was told she would be contacted if needed for further questioning. Time lapsed, a year to be exact, and she heard nothing further from anyone at the Thirty-Third Precinct. She called the precinct and went down there several times, asking for the two detectives on the case and was told they were no longer affiliated with the Thirty-Third Precinct or any for that matter. *What the hell did that mean?* she thought to herself. She even tried to call Niki's mom with the number she last had, which was disconnected. Perhaps it was her mom's way of grieving by disconnecting number and not contacting to give a new one, knowing there were no leads or anything. It was like their murders were swept under the rug. This pained Raven so, thinking it even pushed her into the arms of a tyrant sociopathic sadist that cloaked himself in righteousness, in the righteousness of the OCG.

You are mine and will do as told.

CHAPTER 7

OCG (BRATVA)

New club, new time, new space, thinking this would be good for her if she removed herself from the venue that she danced at with Niki and Britany, a form of compartmentalizing, where one uses this as a defense mechanism to avoid mental/cognitive mental discomfort, suppressing feelings that are hurtful, running away from self again.

Somehow, she met a leader of an OCG (organized crime group) member, Bratva (Russian brotherhood) Vladik, pronounced (Vah-la-dik). He was not a very big man in the stature of a man or in the size of manhood. For some reason, when he locked his eyes on Raven when she was up there on that stage, she became enthralled. Let me tell you, he was in rapture, too curious of the sexy doll dancing in front of him and others up there.

She was adorned in blue, which was her color. As she finished up there, she came down from the stage and took a very large gentleman by the hand and led him into the grandiose silver, white, and red private room for a one-on-one dance. She led him to a red plush couch, given his size. He, in turn, led her to the chair to sit. He barely fit with his stomach pouring over sides and in front of his lap. Raven was finished with that because if he pulled her back, she would feel his dick trying to poke through her thin bikini bottoms, which disgusted her. So as he got comfortable, she sat upon his leg, and they chatted for a couple of minutes until the next song started.

"Ooh, new song," Raven said. Then she got up and began to dance, slowly swaying her hips back and forth and rolling her sexy torso, bouncing her tits in his face on occasion. Then that song ended, and he requested another then another then another until an hour and fifteen minutes had elapsed. She peered over to the doorway and saw Vladik standing there, glaring at her intensely. He was speaking in Russian to his comrades until all three of them were standing there, watching for the next hour. "Oh boy," she said to herself, trying not to make it obvious that she knew he was watching for so long and hard.

When the gentleman she was dancing for was finally finished, it was damn near the time for the club to be closing. Raven escorted the gentleman to the door and gave him a hug. "Thank you. You have made my night and then some. I need to come back and see you again!"

Raven was fine with that and said, "I am looking forward to it. Until then."

Vlad came over to her in full force, saying, "I want you to dance for me *now*!" in his broken English accent. He grabbed her hand very aggressively and took her over to that red velvet couch there. She danced, and they talked as well as he could articulate himself in English, mostly about his name and where he was from. Then Vlad said, "Give me your number, Raven." She quickly obliged. *Hell, why not! This is something different*, not knowing what the fall upon her world was soon to be very poignant. They hung out. He took her to Atlantic City and had what she thought was good sex. Although Raven did think it odd that every time he came to meet her, he wore a bulletproof vest. Flashed back to the night they met and she was going to feel his chest. He grabbed her hands. Now she understood why. The two fell for each other hard, and Raven moved in with Vladik in his small storefront apartment house in Sheepshead Bay. It was a quaint place, mostly brick walls, a fireplace, one bathroom, and a strange-looking kitchen area. It looked as if the appliances weren't for it, just a little hard to explain the details of.

Time went on, and Vlad started to become very possessive and aggressive then abusive. He would go and buy her gifts as an apology for slapping her upside the head/face. It was so hard that her ears would ring for twenty minutes, at least. The first time he struck her was when Raven had gotten mad about how he was talking to her in front of his boys. She walked out, saying, "I'm leaving!" She was speed walking down the sidewalk to the nearby subway station. He caught up to her, grabbed her, and open-palmed her face both sides back to back. Then he began dragging her back to the house, locking her inside behind this steel-industrial door. He pulled down and shut over the main door.

He proceeded to say to her, "You don't walk away from me. You will never leave me unless I tell you to do so. Te ponimayesh, suka?" You understand, bitch? Again, he said, "Te ponimayesh, suka?" Not crying while looking at him, trying to be strong, Raven responded with a *yes*!

He pushed her into the bedroom then locked the bedroom door from the outside. She banged on the door, screaming, "No, Vlad, please open the door! Let me out! I'm sorry!" Raven began to crawl onto the bed and curled up into the pillows as she cried, thinking, *Wow! What true colors are shown very soon. Oh well, this too shall pass.* But lamentably, it did not pass as she thought it would.

Vlad eventually came into the room damn near the next morning, standing in the light of the doorway and just stared at Raven, not saying a word then closing the door. She proceeded to get up, and he came back through the door, grabbing her and hugging her, saying, "I really do sorry!" in his broken English way of speaking. That is the way he would articulate himself and hated it when she tried to correct him. He softly grabbed her face in a coddling manner, kissing her forehead, her nose, her lips, all while still apologizing and saying, "I love you."

Raven forgave him, of course, and they made up, making love well into late morning. As they lay there, she wrapped in his arms, he explained to her his love for her and being of Russian culture, loving hard and deep, possessing all that crosses their path. Vlad also claimed that his grandmother was of Albanian descent. Albanians were strongly emotional-driven creatures, he believed, and that is where his passion is mostly fueled from. Also, her walking away from him and just leaving like that would strike a chord in him to be reactive, not proactive because she belonged to him and him only. This all he needed her to understand and believe more than a hundred percent. Raven did understand and believe every word he said. "Love though?" she said to herself. "I believe he loves me in his own strange way. A sort of arrested love if there can be."

When all this was said and done, Vlad said, "Let's go to Russkaya banya [Russian bathhouse]," a place of exotic saunas, pool, dining area inside with tasty authentic Russian foods with a bar and massage rooms.

Always in hues of blues and greens, so it would add to the tranquil exotic experience one is supposed to have. They proceeded to get up to shower and get dressed, making their way over to the banya.

As they sat there in the bathhouse at one of the dining tables, one of the workers came up to Raven, placing a box right in front of her. "Of course, another lavish present from Vlad," she said to herself. She half smiled and proceeded to open the gift. Inside was a beautiful Cartier watch. Vlad came up behind her and whispered in her ear, "You do love it?"

Raven paused then said, "Yes, it is gorgeous, Vladik, thank you!"

He put the watch on her wrist as some food he had ordered was brought to their area—an array of cheeses, meats, fish, veggies, and delicious fresh-pressed juices from apple to a cucumber mix. They ate, they laughed, they talked, and all was well.

More time eventually passed during which they went to different restaurants, nightclubs. It was all things forgotten it seemed, although she would remember everything—every striking emotional hit from the words he would use to cut her down, not to mention the force of his blows to her physically. Vlad would always have Raven by his side dressed to a tea in the upper echelon of apparel, jewelry, and shoes. His hot spot was Romanoff in Brooklyn, on good old Coney Island Avenue formally Rasputin's, where they would have cabaret shows.

One night, Raven was there with Vladik and his crew. As they were wrapping up their evening, some man approached Raven, implying to put his hand around her waist, explaining how beautifully sexy she was. Vladik snapped as he came up closer to the man's face, both exchanging banter in Russian. Vladik grabbed the man by his throat, literally dragging him toward the staircase of the front door then outside and beat him to a pulp. There were blood and teeth all on the stairs outside and on the sidewalk from Vlad kicking him, slamming his face into the concrete. All this vulgar display of power by Vladik showed to be unpropitious for that poor Russian fool of a man. This took place right across from the Sixtieth Precinct. The police did nothing. They would come out and watch different events of such took place, making bets on who would win. For some reason, they had disquietude of Vladik that seemed to grow by the minute. He knew this and took full advantage of it, abusing his power whenever he seemed fit to do so. They knew of his lifestyle, his illegal dealings, as did Raven for the most part. So it didn't really make her much better than the officers.

Oh, and when they went home, she got it bad from Vlad. He beat her upside the face until black, blue, and purple, yelling at Raven in Russian, in English for being too sexy and attractive, yet he admired that and showcased her as his most prized possession. It took a few days before she was healed, except for a few bruises. This time, she thought of a plan to fix him good, saying to herself, "You want to beat me?"

One night, she was there at the house alone and found one of his favorite guns tucked away, a beautiful Glock with a solid gold trigger made in Chechnya. She awaited him to return and get undressed and comfortable down to just his boxers and socks. Raven sat in the corner of the room, and as he walked in, she pulled it on him and told him not to move. She proceeded to pick up the phone like she was calling in an arrest, sounding very convincing like she was undercover on a sting op. Easy for her, she learned from her uncle that was a sergeant at the Seventy-Second Precinct in Sunset Park, Brooklyn. Well, at least when he was around and would tell her stories. Vladik fell for it, believing he was under surveillance this entire time they had been together. Have you seen a man shake in his boxers and socks before? It was a wonderful sight to see for Raven. She relished in it, having him right by the fucking balls. "Not so much of a tough guy now, huh, Vlad?" Raven needed to do this to assert control over the situation, hoping to make him rethink his ways, especially with her.

She said to him, "Remember that night you and your goons grabbed that guy from around the corner on Kings Highway and put him in an industrial trash bag, beating him to a pulp inside the basement, leaving him in for days alone, suffering? Just to let you know that was a cop, or did you know that?"

Vladik said, "Yes, yes, I did know that. He was in my pocket!"

"Well, he was found shot with one bullet straight to the head execution-style." Vlad swallowed and swallowed hard and deep. Not that he was in shock of the death of the cop but more so of Raven's knowledge of the situation. He said, "How in the fuck do you know this, Raven? Who are you *really*?"

She just smiled and began to snicker, which showed to be a bit of a mistake being she got too comfortable in turn, giving him a chance to run for it. That is exactly what Vlad did. He took off like a bat out the hell out the front door in the middle of winter, snow covering the ground. It was fucking cold outside. New York could have some cold-ass winters at times. All in his little boxers and socks, he ran out in it. It was quite funny to her, and she laughed so hard, saying, "Yes, yes, I got that fucker!" Then she started to think, *Shit, he's going to come back with a vengeance, either alone or with his Bratva.* So she began to panic, then the phone rang. "Oh fuck!"

There is a saying that you can lead a horse to water, but you cannot make it drink. Here goes the beginning of the end.

Fast-forward some, and they moved down to Florida in a lavish home, decked out with the finest Italian furniture, a maid, groundskeeper, you name it. They also got engaged down in Florida on the beach. Every girl's and guy's, maybe, fantasy, yes? She had gotten pregnant with a boy named Dimitri, little Dima, for short, named after his grandfather.

Vlad started to force Raven's hand into making up drug packages for FedEx for shipment to Florida, Moscow, etc. One day, she came to Vladik and wanted to speak with him regarding her going back to dancing. Abhorrently against it, he struck her, saying, "You want to dance, you want to go back dancing? Wasn't it enough your two friends being slaughtered like farmhouse pigs?"

Raven was like, "Fuck you, Vlad! You're a piece of shit. Matter a fact, you ain't shit."

Vlad continued rambling on, saying, "Are you not the mother of my son? You're the mother of my son, but I will change that quickly fast!" Keep in mind, his English was not the best. He then struck her again repeatedly until she hit the floor, kicking her in her stomach and her back down the hallway, moving her at least a foot with each blow until she blacked out. What she did really know at that point was she was out cold.

Waking back up, she had blood leaking from every orifice, peeing herself. He put her in the bath because she could barely walk and bathed her, trying to look in her eyes, which were swollen shut on a face blown up from getting beaten upside it so hard. Once again, "I really do sorry," he said in his broken English way. He took her out of the bath, dried her off, moisturized her up, put her in one of her nightgowns, and put her in the bed. Again, he was coming in and staring at her in the doorway as if he was admiring his work in a very sadistic way. She felt as if there wasn't a thing she could do until that day…a presence of mind in a hellish time.

CHAPTER 8

THE PRESENCE OF MIND

The presence was overwhelming. Vlad had to go up to New York for his "so-called" business dealings. He packed down the Acura and told Raven of his departure. Upon telling her, she felt an ominous presence come over her but relief as well. He kissed her goodbye, then proceeded to get into the car, and left for the drive. Raven stayed alone for a while as his parents would always have Dima. As she awaited his arrival in New York, she just finished nursing up her own wounds and trying to heal right from the previous beating by Vladik, the parasite. She really began to hate him profusely. She would say, "You tell me you love me so you can have your justification for beating me to a bloody fucking pulp." She was trying to fully process all this hellishness in her life, but she just couldn't. It made her sick. She just kneed inside. She had to muster up strength somehow from somewhere. She had no one to really turn to. She was in this fight alone. Where is the justice? Does it even exist?

A week and a half had passed by, and Raven researched ways of trying to escape the clutches of this tyrant she had fallen in love with at one point. Suddenly, the phone rang. It was Vladik, telling her she needed to come to New York and bring up $30,000 with her. He told her how to withdraw a said amount then directed her to where the keys are to the safe deposit box at the bank. She hurried readily and got a bag of clothing together and other necessities. She headed to the bank quickly, knowing they would be closing soon. The entire time she was driving, she was thinking, *This could be my moment, my moment of escape from this hellish life at the same time wiping him out of everything.* Logic came into play, causing the realistic thought that if she did such a thing, he would find her and remove her head from her body. She shook it off while approaching the bank to do as commanded. She headed back to the house to get online to book a flight. In luck, there was one departing that evening, the last flight of the day. Vlad's mother already had their son at her house, which was a relief. She organized the money in a bag layered in clothing and called to make sure she arrived in NYC. She was greeted at arrivals by some new goon she had never met before named Anatoly. He said, "You can call me Tony, the other Russian Albanian." Then he laughed menacingly.

It was 30 degrees below out, fucking wintertime again, and this dude was wearing a wifebeater tank with two clearly evident star tattoos on his shoulder, and inside his forearm was a double eagle tattoo. Raven said to herself, "Oh shit! This guy is something serious." As he was leading her to the car and took her bags, she was brainstorming what in the fuck do the star tattoos mean. "I've seen them before. Come on, Raven! Think! Goddamn it." It finally clicked high status of some sort, a type of captain within Russian mafia. So he was Russian and Albanian, it seems.

From what she knew, the two nationalities were some sort of rivals. Well, maybe, she wasn't sure now. It was all hearsay anyway. Perhaps what the fuck. He was the guy at the basement party that ordered the hooker for the dog. At the same time, her phone rang. It was Vlad, telling her Tony was to take her over to Brooklyn where he is and not to be startled by his fierce-looking first impression.

"Too late," she said to herself while shaking her head.

He said, "I love you. See you soon!" She hung up the phone, not giving a reply to his bullshit I love you remark.

Tony said not another word to Raven upon the drive as she sat in the back seat, where he put her. He would just occasionally stare at her through the rearview mirror, like studying her, watching her. His eyes were staring deeply into hers then to her lips. Then he would lick his lips. After that, he would stare down at her breasts. She did not react. She just turned her head and pulled her coat tightly closed, saying, "Another cold New York winter, huh?" Tony still had no reply. Raven said to herself, "This guy is a fucking weirdo. Leave it to Vlad though. He can find the best of them."

They eventually got to an apartment in Brooklyn. He took her out of the car, escorted her upstairs, and there was Vladik, awaiting her arrival. She walked in, acting as if happy to see him. She had to play the part because she knew she had to get away somehow. She prayed on it. Vladik, the parasite, he was just cold and stoic.

Vlad, Jorik, and Slav went into the kitchen to discuss transactions about some drug deal after Vlad had a quick word with Anatoly, that fucking weirdo Tony guy before Tony was leaving out.

Upon coming out of the kitchen, he told her his parents were coming up with the baby for the weekend for some Russian troop show. She said, "That's fine as long as he has all he needs to stay warm."

Suddenly, Vlad started yelling uncontrollably and loud and brash, then he came to Raven, demanding she got on the phone and tracked some packages quickly. He was emphatically telling her, "If you do not do as instructed, you will be limping around here in Brooklyn from me beating you again."

Never seems to end, she thought to herself. He was breaking her down in such a condescending manner and in front of his boys, who just looked away.

She put her head down and once again quickly obliged to Vlad's demand. Night soon came, and with the night, so did his parents with little Dima. They came, and Vlad gave his father an envelope filled with cash she was sure, and then they soon left. At least Dima had been bathed and fed well. Raven went to put him to bed and crawled up next to him to sleep. A single tear ran down her cheek, and while she was wishing and wanting an escape, she just couldn't see how.

As the night passed on till late night, she heard a noise and indistinctive chattering. She exited the bedroom, and Slav was saying on camera he saw what looked like the police, and he thought they had surrounded the building. Oh, they did more than that. They cut the signal there on the roof then took to the front door with a battering ram. It was SWAT for sure. Vlad quickly came to her, telling her to put the leftover money in the baby bag. By that time, they had already gained entry into the apartment. She moved swiftly though, already had grabbed the watches and cash, and stashed it.

"Get down on the floor," they yelled! She didn't because she was holding the baby. Vladik, Jorik, and Slav got on the floor, and DTs grabbed them one by one and searched them then handcuffed them. A female officer took Raven into the bathroom and strip-searched her. She allowed her to get dressed fully because she was wearing nothing but a tank top and shorts. She got Dima all wrapped up to go, then the officer escorted her outside, where there were three paddy wagon-like vans awaiting with the back of the doors open for some reason. She thought it was to make them suffer because it was brutally cold out, dead of winter. They placed her in one of the vans that Vlad was not in, mostly filled with other goons. Some she recognized. Others she had not.

One of the detectives said to her, "Raven, we are going to give you a chance to bring your child somewhere safe. Is there a nearby relative or close friend you can entrust his well-being with?" She knew she only had one chance and knew his parents were long gone.

Thinking to herself, *I got to figure this out quickly, for they are telling me my child will be lost in the system if not forever for a very long time to come.* She could think of only one person, Gia, and gave the officer the number to call. She answered thank heavens, where she quickly explained to her the goings-on. On the way down to booking, they stopped over in the Park Slope area of Brooklyn. Two of the officers escorted her to the door, where Gia opened up and quickly took Dima in. A sigh of relief came over Raven because she knew Vlad was going to be gone but also a cloud of fear—an intense fear of the not knowing. She proceeded to get back in the van. Now they handcuffed her wrists and ankles like everyone else.

Finally, they arrived at the precinct, guys first taken out and she last. They brought her to an isolated area where three detectives questioned her for about five hours, relentless in their attack, for there was no good cop bad cop. They were ruthless. They were threatening her with a twenty-five to life sentence, saying she, in fact, was the orchestrator in the cop being killed. They showed her ten-inch thick profile mugshot books of many gang-affiliated members—Bratva and Mug, which are terms used by Albanian for a gangster.

There were even pictures of her sending and receiving packages of drug paraphernalia. Then came the ace, a photo of her dressed outside of Romanoff's, where this cop that had been killed grabbed her by the arm, pulling her in closely in a very sexual manner then her slapping his face. She was stunned at all but most of the detail of that photo and how closely she was even being watched. Then one of the officers got up and struck her so hard that she flew out of the chair into the wall. Her face clearly busted open.

He said, "Is this what you like, yes?" Then he went in for more right before another officer grabbed him, demanding him to stop.

Raven began to laugh loudly and uncontrollably, saying, "No, this is what you like. This is what gets your little prick hard, you son of a bitch." Then she spit out blood and looked up at him. "How does it feel to become the very thing you hate the very thing you loathe?" She knew in her heart he was no better than Vlad or any man that could raise his hand to a woman. She knew that he knew the beatings she endured from Vladik. This made her sick to her stomach. The beating went on though like she was a dog's hooker.

CHAPTER 9

A DOG AND HIS HOOKER

For instance, a dog and a hooker of Jorik—as she was sitting and listening to one of the detectives that were in the illegal gambling hall that night undercover, everything started to play back from that night in her head very vividly. This was something unlike anything other, anything other than Raven had ever seen. She really had seen some shit. She thought until this. Of course, why wouldn't the detectives know all about this night of illegal gambling in the Coney Island basement where Jorik ordered a hooker to boost the excitement and get more people to come and gamble? So the hooker came, and Jorik set her up to fuck his dog Bogdin, a Dogue de Bordeaux, also known as a French mastiff, very powerful and muscular in its look.

In any event on this lovely hot summer night, a hooker came to the underground casino, a quaint place with actual gambling tables, dealers, and all. Walls were red with black trim, plush chairs to ensure your comfort so you'd stay longer. There was dim lighting in a very smoke-filled atmosphere. As far as the hooker, who just stood over on the side, waiting patiently with her long blond wig on, it seemed she was a stunningly sexy-looking thing, not very tall, petite with large breasts—breasts that would barely stay in her bikini top. Her nipples were as hard as walnut shells but the size of grapes at least. "How in the hell are her nipples that large?" Raven thought to herself!

Jorik announced what was about to take place, "Gentlemen and few ladies, I'm now to present my dog dancing show. I am sure you will take delight in it, and if not, I'll just break your fucking faces." He then laughed, shaking his head, and Vlad was laughing with him. You could hear a deep breath from the crowd when out she came, a hooker dressed in a crotchless bikini. She was pretty fine, that was for sure, even with her wearing a long blond wig, which cascaded down on her glowing chocolate skin. She had started dancing and gyrating all over then on the floor. Soon Jorik walked up with Boris, his dog, a huge dog in its stature. It looked like a fighter dog; therefore, Boris was fitting.

There was a long pole attached from floor to ceiling, known as a stripper pole. She did a trick, turning herself upside down where her pussy was exposed, and then Jorik walked up and started eating her pussy. He then whistled, commanded Boris, his dog, that got on his hind legs and did pretty much the same. Yes. There it was said. He licked her there. She then flipped down, dancing and still gyrating and all.

Smoke and strobe lights came on. As she leaned against the stripper pole, Boris literally sniffed her ass and between her legs. Jorik put his hand right between her legs, making a "come hither" motion. He then turned her around so she would be facing the pole while Boris leaned on his hind paws. After which, he was mounting her while Jorik was still standing right there at this point with a glove on his hand, directing the dog's penis into the hooker.

He then stepped back, watching like everybody else. Raven did not enjoy that disgusting ass shit. She thought it to be despicable. She looked around at everyone else with their eyes locked, most in excitement and others in shock but no disgust. There was even a guy that had his junk out, jerking off to it. *What the fuck is going on?* she thought. *There is a dog in front of him fucking a hooker. He has not apparently received that bestiality memo where it is not okay, where it is not acceptable for a dog and a human female or male, for that matter, to have intercourse.*

It was absolutely not okay. It was fucking repulsive. Then you heard the hooker state, "He's clawing me bad. It feels like he's ripping my skin." She tried to pull away, and Boris let out this deep hard growl then bit her neck to hold her still—not drawing blood though, which was amazing. Jorik said something indistinct in Russian. Perhaps it was Albanian to Boris, hard to tell. Then Boris just froze. I mean, he stopped in midfuck of this hooker. Holy shit! That was some power in command. Jorik and one of his goons grabbed some socks and placed them on Boris's front paws before telling him to commence again. This was one of the most compelling things ever to have taken place—a dog just steadily fucking a hooker, going at it so savagely. Believe it or not, she also seemed to be liking it, as long as she wasn't getting clawed up. Raven stood bewildered and nauseated. She still could not remove her eyes from this perversion any more than twenty-five feet away from her.

Then suddenly, there was a deep grumble of a sound with an undertone of moaning. Boris ejaculated profusely! There was a puddle of dog semen on the floor everywhere, around the stripper pole and all. At that point, Raven walked off swiftly to a nearby restroom and vomited upon opening of the door. This made her sick as all hell. She kept saying to herself, "I didn't just watch that. I didn't just witness that, did I?" Over and over, she said this to herself, as if in a chant to reverse, maybe what she saw just happened.

She cleaned herself up and proceeded to go back out, playing it off as if she was just fine. As she was walking back over, she saw Vlad collect a handful of cash from Jorik. She was not really paying attention until more people were collecting or he was giving them. There was so much going on. She put two and two together and realized this was a fucking bet with her Vlad involved in the entire shit.

Then she looked over at the pole as the room cleared a little. She saw two guys and a girl with mops and two buckets. They were mopping up the dog semen, boatloads of it.

She said to Vlad, "Why, why, and how could you partake in something of this, this?" trying to think of a proper word to use in English so he wouldn't think she was trying to berate him and be conflictive. "There is no decency in this sort of thing, Vlad. It is bestiality at its lowest form—in any form. I'm only telling you this because I love you," which she did more so because she felt sorry for him.

Suddenly, he grabbed Raven by the throat. Jorik just watched and actually laughed a little, saying, "Kontrollin e asaj laviree."

That was definitely Albanian and derogatory, Raven thought. Then Vlad went in, showing as he was to kiss her and headbutted her. She then fell limp in his arms as he held her close. Vladik then said to Jorik, "Yes, I must control my whore. You're right." She heard everything even when being dizzied from the blow. Yet she accepted his advance of holding her close and stayed calm. What the hell else could she do? He had his enforcer right there, and there was no telling what they would have done to her further. So she held him back but didn't cry, no sobbing at all. She knew as much as she hated him, she did have love for him, but how?

What a disturbingly dysfunctional, sordid affair between these two. It was toxicity at its finest for Raven. She knew she had to pull away. She knew this was a living hell. "Do people have it worse somewhere? Maybe," she said at the point where if she even had a thought of defying Vladik, he would end her life with a snap of a finger. Unfortunately, she was stuck. Or so it seemed in the unveiling of time.

CHAPTER 10

UNVEILING OF TIME

Time was a real thing. In the unveiling of time, not all was what it seemed. So much evidence was brought to hand in court that Vlad had no leg to stand on. He got twenty-five years. Jorik turned and got only three years and Slava, six. There was a talk that Jorik was making moves with other nationalities, the Albanians. Who knows though? People always have something to say.

A few others got three, five, and the ones with no time definitely turned evidence and most likely ended up in WITSEC since the case went federal with all the state line crossing offenses—state-to-state prostitution and trafficking.

Raven received only five years of probation, a miracle within itself. She thought for sure she was done for even after doing only six months in a woman's lockup, where everyone adored her and didn't want her to leave. She became really good friends with an inmate in lockup named Nicole, whom she took a strong liking to, and they became good friends. They exchanged stories of despicable tragic events that they endured. Plus, Nicole closely resembled her friend Niki, who was murdered earlier in her life. Pretty sure that made the connection even stronger. She missed her crazily.

There was a night though when the two of them talked at length. This night, in particular, was a pivotal moment for Raven. Nicole told Raven a story in vivid detail when she was fifteen years old and met a guy on the Internet. A thing called Black Page.

She was to fly back into Louisiana from Oakland, and her dad was supposed to pick her up. Instead, she told this guy she met via the Internet, who lived there, and he said he would pick her up. She waited at the airport briefly, and he came, looking nothing like his photo, but she thought to herself, *Well, that's the Internet* pic, I guess. She then got in the car, and he started acting very strangely and twitching and stuff. He was driving out of the way like toward a boondocks-looking area surrounded by sugarcane fields out in Saint John's Parish. He then pulled over when they were completely surrounded by the fields, and he dragged her out of the car, grabbed her, and started beating her repeatedly. He ripped her overall short, set off, pinned her on the car, ripped her panties, then proceeded to rape her violently. He then went to pull handcuffs out, and when she saw this, she saw it as a moment to escape, which she did.

Running into the sugarcane fields, she heard him driving around in the car, looking for her and screaming. "Nicole, get your hot little ass back over here *now*!" She stayed down low, hiding and trying to make her way to the highway nearby. With one flip-flop, a bra and panties all ripped, she made her way to the highway, collapsing right in front of someone driving an 18-wheeler. The gentleman exited from the truck, went to ask her what happened, "Are you okay?" Realizing no response and blood coming down her inner thigh, he picked her up, covering her with a sweatshirt of his, and put her in the truck, alerting police and driving her to a nearby hospital.

There at the hospital, he gave his name and how he found her. They had to do a thorough investigation rape kit and all on her and even test the trucker. They found semen, but it was no match to him. At the hospital, her uncle was contacted to pick her up and came to retrieve her. Shortly before, she had been locked up in the women's facility. He was seeking her out on the Internet, acting as if nothing took place and wanted to see her. Nicole decided to do it to exact her revenge. She said, "Revenge is what I had, all I had. I told him I wanted to meet at a motel, and he came, and I wanted him to have the handcuffs, which he brought, but he wasn't counting on me having acid in a polyethylene bottle. I poured it all over his nasty ass dick. Should have heard the screams and cries of him like the little bitch he truly was." Nicole knew that he would get a slap on the wrist if even so decided to wait it out and exact revenge in her own way. This, in turn, landed her in lockup, but five years was worth it to her, which she would only do half the time having another year left.

Nicole was a pretty thing, much too pretty to be locked up in jail. She did the crime and got caught to have to do time. As cliché as it might sound, it was true.

As Raven listened to her telling the perils of what she had gone through, she didn't have any pity for her. In fact, she was admiring and giving her food for thought in a strengthening manner, knowing that if she had to, she would do it again, maybe a little differently but yet again. She felt as if men had a strong chauvinistic side to them. Well, most men, the demeaning and sexist—most definitely under-developed in their punitive, primitive minds.

Deep in thought, Raven soaked it all in as Nicole told her story of that time of hell.

Leopards do no change their spots overnight, a lesson well learned, a powerful silent movement of events to make order out of chaos, enduring what must be to move to the next level, leading to the visits with a parasite.

CHAPTER 11

THE PARASITE

The parasite still had Raven in his clutch. Raven was as she was still in deep with Vlad feeling as if she owed him something of herself. For he was a great manipulator, needing her now more than ever but for purely selfish reasons. She was like smuggling pills in for him with weed and money to have on hand for bartering inside. She did kind of get off going there, dressing very sexy but classy, especially in summerlike. She was old-world Hollywood royalty. As much as he hated it, he loved it too because he knew every man in that visiting area plus the COs wanted to fuck her. To let him see her out and sexy as all hell was another way to ease the pain for her and to cause it for him.

Unfortunately, she would go and visit and sometimes take Gia with her, who would see Slava. Her heart wasn't in it even before the lockup. She just felt like she had a duty to be there.

Dima was safe with his parents. They were raising him and really didn't want her or allow her around him. *It is better for little Dima to have them in his life*, she thought. His parents became very menacing and threatening, and she knew that Vlad was behind it, instructing them to be that way toward her. They believed their son being locked away was her fault, and she didn't fight it. The only reason why his mother ever intervened when he beat Raven if she was around was that the baby would be nearby or in the room.

In any event, she'd go and visit the piece of shit over and over. She even went dancing at another high-end strip club to get an extra

$10,000 together to give a lawyer for him. She sold the watches as he instructed and took that money for him too. They had nothing left back in their house in Florida. As soon as news broke about the arrest in New York, the house was ransacked, and everything of value was taken, even the dogs and her cat. So there was nothing.

Another day came when Raven went in to visit Vlad again, where he gave her some papers to push that they would get married. This scared the living hell out of her, especially his urgency to do it so quickly now when he had ample opportunity to do so when out. She said to herself, "What the hell is his motive? Bingo, conjugal visits. Oh fuck!"

"Stop giving him so much of you and relinquishing all your control to this piece of shit. For he is a piece of shit." She knew in her heart he was behind the cop being murdered. Why else would he have kept him in a cellar and torture and beat him for the time period he did? Not to mention him literally kicking her down the hallway, him beating her so hard that she fell through a window, him having sex with her sister and lying about it when she was recovering from childbirth. There was so much, so much that could and should not have happened nor be forgotten. She silently enjoyed him suffering being locked up but would not ever show it. Such silent pleasures!

Thinking back in time to the times, some good but mostly bad—the torture she saw of other members of his crew, of nonmembers, of herself being beaten beyond recognition at times, even as close cohorts stood or sat or watched or listened. She knew that she really loved him and gave her all and to have to be brought to this. It wasn't right. It wasn't normal, and it resonated so deeply all the time. She was utterly afraid to really try to move ahead, thinking it would bleed off onto what she would try to do or be with.

No choice though. He was locked away for many good reasons, and there was no time like the present to make an escape that was so overdue. "No looking back. Not now for what?" she said to herself. "I must take this and not let it be done in vain all that from even the teen years. Don't let it define you. Let yourself grow, and maybe, just maybe, there will be a silver lining."

She was still friends with a girl she danced with at various spots, who told her about the promise of Vegas and starting a new. They would have discussions about a lot of things from sex, dancing for different men, the other girls at the clubs, and sex with dark entities. Oliviette was something, I tell you. She found this out even more so when she stayed over at Oliviette's place for a minute.

For example, one night, O, as she was called often, was being taken sexually by what she referenced as a dark spirit or entity.

She swore that an ex of hers, a Haitian lover named Kervans, this man she described as being tall, handsome, with dark chocolate glistening skin and hazel-colored eyes.

He had a bald head with a scar on his face as if some sort of branding mark. She said that Kervans was the one that put the dark entity on her because they parted ways, and he told her he'd never let her go. "Oh well," she said, followed up with a "Here's Vegas, baby."

What happens in Vegas stays in Vegas.

So it is said.

There is another world behind all those glitzy lights.

CHAPTER 12

VEGAS, BABY

Vegas, baby, there she went. He let her go with no choice in the matter. Raven left and went out to Vegas with her girlfriend, Oliviette, she danced with. She figured overall, it would be better for her to be there, and she had no reason to stay out east anymore, especially having Dima taken away from her by his parents anyway.

Raven liked to call her Olive because she was tall with olive skin but much curvier than the Olive Oyl character from *Popeye*. They always called her O in the club. A strong throwback look to Lena Horne is truly what she was.

They racked up on some money, living good and having so much just thrown at them. They both felt as if Vegas was the place to be. Working long nights though, they quickly turned into early mornings. They met people from all walks of life, actors, singers, rappers, some fighters, you name it.

That was one thing Raven never wanted to be part of. She did not like the celebrity-like world of those characters, as she said, always thinking too shallow. And their self-centered, self-entitlement lifestyle and way of thinking was a bore.

Olive thought to the contrary and simply adored all of it. She even started dating a rapper of high status, who she would never kiss. Always thinking that to be odd, Raven finally was like, "Why? Kissing is the fundamental of any good relationship. It tells a lot about a person, their qualities, etc."

Olive stated, "No, it's not that. It's the sex. You must jump right in and have the sex to see because that is the determining factor. Preferably anal!"

What? Raven thought to herself. *I love this dear friend of mine, but she has completely lost her fucking mind.*

Olive said, "The first night I met with my rapper man, we had sex on the bathroom hotel floor, and it was anal."

So Raven said, "You let a complete stranger stick his dick into your ass before even kissing him? That is fucking nasty, O."

"Yes, I did, and it might be gross to some people, but it is what it is. We were both willing participants," Olive responded.

This was definitely something Raven could not wrap her brain around, not so much of her past of rape and incestuous moments, but it was just so foreign and sounded ridiculously painful and scary— plus, her tranny friends back in New York and their complaints of "loose-booty syndrome." *Well,* she thought to herself, *everybody has their thing, and I guess that is Olive's thing.* "Have fun with that, I guess, O!"

Now time passed, and Olive and her man were dating heavily. She even left Vegas to move out to Agoura Hills in California to live with him. Oh boy! Everything was going fine until they had a huge fight, and he tried throwing her out. She demanded he give her at least $10,000 because they were together a couple of years, and she footed the bill for moving expenses.

She eventually left then came back to live with Raven. While there, he called repeatedly, trying to talk and be caring and say sorry. You know, the whole shit dumbass guys go through when they realized they fucked up and lost a good thing. They made up for some god-awful reason, and he apparently wanted to talk to me on the phone and asked for me to come with her to his house for a cookout party. "Hell, no!"

Thank you, but no thank you, I thought to myself. He was just recently cussed out by me on the phone.

In any event, Raven and Olive started to get ready for work that evening. Olive adorned in black as always and Raven in her blue, her favorite color. The club was packed. It was a Saturday night, wall-to-wall patrons just grabbing, wanting dances, and waiting patiently for such. Raven made her way off the stage and into the private back room of plush couches in black and thick green plush carpeting with the smell of amber in the air. She literally spent five hours back there with one patron at $400 an hour. You do the math. As it started getting later into the night, another dancer came into the back room with a patron and began dancing for him, which was the norm. Suddenly, at one point, an hour and a half in, the dancer started riding the patron. His dick was exposed and everything. Raven was in shock and was trying to block the view of the patron she was with so he would not see and think he was ripped off. "Holy shit, what the fuck am I supposed to do now?"

Refusing to ever fuck for her money and sometimes going out on dates and dating guys and not wanting to fuck them at all made her sick to her stomach.

She was just constantly thinking to herself, *If he sees this, I'm done*, and he just said he wanted to stay another three hours. Right when she saw his face turn and almost get a full visual of what was happening, she bent down, put her face in his, and kissed him ever so passionate as she could. Well, it actually worked in her favor because from that point on, he just wanted to have her sit with him and have some drinks and still pay her for her time.

Things like that just do not happen as such. Luck of the draw. Vegas, baby. Oh, Vegas, baby! Well, it did, and it continued over several months on and off working there. His name was Jonathan with a two-inch penis, literally, well, maybe three, but that was being kind. She found this out after she allowed herself to eventually go out on some dates with him and making out.

She could not allow herself to go any further, fearful that it would be a lost cause due to the minuscule size of it. She did not want to be emasculating to him, for he was kind to her. It would eventually fade out. You know, when the contact gets more and more scarce, fade away for the better. Raven knew that it could only go so far for so long.

The mutual attraction of the two was not that mutual. It was completely one-sided, and that started to take a toll on Raven. She wanted something real. She knew what it felt like to just be taken advantage of and didn't want to put that out there. It came back, you know.

She watched how these other women would just do and say whatever to these men, just taking them for suckers and taking that cash by any means necessary.

For it was an ongoing vicious cycle of money, seeking lust without love, without even kindness and care. She always believed there was common decency to be somehow in the club world. She would say, "I don't want to strip without a conscience." Inside, if anyone could just be stoic and coldhearted, no conscience, she believed she'd be that one to have that given right. At the same token, you never really know what others have gone through. So that was something she always took into consideration, especially when Kristen disappeared. Oh, the Kristen clawing.

There are bigger things than what we see.

CHAPTER 13

KRISTEN CLAWING

Kristen, the quintessential girl next door, came up as just having vanished, gone without a trace, for about two months straight. She was about five foot six with strawberry curly blond hair with cheek freckles and rosy pink lips and pale skin. She had a sinful cuteness to her.

She usually walked around in pink knee-high socks and pink little spandex bootie shorts or just a thong. She liked to walk around topless in the back, smoking out of apples too. She was trying to be inconspicuous, saying, "It gives it a nice smell." In fact, it did to the point that several didn't even know she was smoking meth out of those apples though it was just marijuana. "All right, I guess. If you like it, I love it then." That was just her thing perhaps, and she didn't like or want to even try to pass judgment on it, for it wasn't her place. Everyone has got their thing, right?

She had some sort of thing all right that when the detectives suddenly came into the club to question a bunch of us girls and the housemother, who is a lady, usually an older ex-dancer that comforts the girls, that makes sure they have food in the back of the house, snacks, drinks, toiletries, and mentors them. She would be tipped by each at the end of their shifts. There is most likely one in every high-end establishment, such as The Wild Horse.

She was definitely older but sexy with tattoos, very tanned skin, fierce deep-blue eyes, probably more so because her skin was so tanned, not sure. She had large breasts, thin hips, and thin legs. Her name was Hinto-Dolly, which was definitely a partial Native

American name. She always wore jeans and a grime wifebeater tank. For some reason, they looked like she rolled them in tobacco. Possibly, she just liked them like that. She was sincere in her kindness and always smelled good though, considering she did smoke like a chimney.

When detectives showed up asking questions, some of the girls spoke very openly about Kristen, from being a lesbian to doing drugs to fucking for money with absolutely no empathy, and others, as Raven, expressed concern out of care, showing too much empathy. Raven knew of Kristen's drug use, and she knew of her promiscuity, especially when high and drunk. She did wonder how she could allow herself to do the things she saw. For instance, the episode in the private room when Raven was with Jonathan, trying to divert his attention. Remember? Well, that was her, and now she was gone.

"Apparently, her mother put her out as missing," the detective said. Mrs. Kavowitz had not heard from her daughter as often as she normally did in the past. This alerted her to make contact with her roommate, who told her mother of Kristen's dancing at this gentlemen's establishment. All along, she thought that she was just a caretaker in Vegas for a well-to-do family that worked ungodly hours. Think of the shocking feeling she felt when she found out her only daughter was stripping in Vegas. *Oh my god! Poor, Kristen*, Raven thought to herself. *Please, please pop up, married or pregnant—something of the sort to ease her mother's heartbreak at least.*

Nobody knew what Mrs. Kavowitz looked like because no one had met her before. More time began to lapse, and still no trace of Kristen. No phone calls either. A missing person's flyer had been made, and several were placed around the city. A bunch of us girls got together one night when we were off to eat sushi and drink sake since most of us were housed in the same place. Conveniences perhaps. We all dressed cute for the most part, except for Monica, the loud and boisterous one of us all, who hated Kristen. She had to put some extras on it.

Monica, the same height as Kristen with dark hair and very pale skin with her little pink tight skirt dress on, saw one of the flyers of Kristen on a streetlight pole and ripped it off while calling Kristen every name in the book, threw it to the ground, and stepped on it with her stiletto heel. Then she asked us to stand around her as she squatted down and pissed on Kristen's flyer. This was easy enough for her to do, given she wasn't wearing any panties. Even if she were, she would have removed them and did it anyway.

Raven refused to stand there and join in. Then she and Kimber just walked on to the side, talking as if they didn't even hear Monica's demand. Very pretty in her way, Monica was. It was just her fucked-up ugly ass personality that overshadowed her looks, much to her dismay because everyone always wanted to kick her ass, though most did nothing, and she always counted on that.

"Anyway, it was a fun night of sushi, sake, dancing the stress away. Dancing for just our fucking enjoyment, not for money and sexual favors for fucked guys," Monica said.

Everything was a joke to her, even the disappearance of Kristen. Even gentlemen in the club, everyone, or thing that crossed her path, she would disrespect. Oh, and the men, even if not in the club, she would emasculate them. Raven thought to herself, *Damn, if only this bitch had met and known Vlad. He'd have her reevaluating life.* Raven began to really like Monica as a friend. It was just her mouth that would get under your skin.

Okay, sidetracked, back to the thought of Vladik, Not to take his side with anything, but he was just very forcefully controlling in that regard to the point you wouldn't really even know it. Definitely a great manipulator he was. Raven blinked as she talked to herself, shaking her head, saying, "Stop it, Raven. Don't you dare give that tyrant one more thought after all he did you." Then just like that, the thought of his dumbass was gone.

Some people were just very coldhearted up inside. Monica had deep-seated jealousy of Kristen because Kristen had this seductive girl-next-door nature about her, and gents in the club would flock to her over Monica. It made one wonder if Monica had anything to do with Kristen's disappearance. This was speculation of many of us that worked there. It was just something that wasn't ever mentioned outside of the small circle of us. Yet Raven challenged Monica that night on, saying to her, "I and a lot of us have known that you loathed

Kristen from the bottom of your heart, Monica, and now she's gone, taken like a thief in the night."

Monica had nothing much to say for herself except that "You, Raven, and everyone else can go fuck yourself."

Monica was one for letting the alcohol speak for her. Finally, Monica saw that she could not intimidate Raven as she always had everyone else. She thought to the contrary with Raven because she always stayed quiet and to herself, especially since she was not so much in the house anymore. If one thing Raven learned after her years of abuse from Vlad was to fight and protect herself well by any means necessary. Plus, back home, she and Gia would do slap-boxing matches at the Russian boxing gym. Raven also knew that people like that had to be eventually checked, or they would constantly be all mouthy and menacing.

"Now you can go fuck yourself and you." She basically started pointing at them all. Well, you can lie to others, but you can't lie to yourself. Funny how no one else sitting at the table would dare to bring it up. Raven didn't care. She stood her ground, waiting for Monica to jump up in her face as she did and then tried swinging on Raven, missing, of course. Then Raven just open palmed her across the face, causing her to fall directly on her ass. Slight chuckling was heard in the background as Monica lay on the ground, holding her cheek, saying, "You hit me. You fucking cunt bitch, you hit me."

Raven said, "Yes, I did, but you got up in my face in a threatening manner, trying to hit me, which is so damned stupid. Therefore, we are even, you fucking bitch."

Monica helped herself up off the floor with no assistance from any of the girls. She approached Raven again, this time, apologizing wholeheartedly. Then they all did some sake shots together, laughed it off, and danced. Things always managed to work their way out among friends—I mean, if they are truly friends. After all, the two did become roommates after some time out of most of all the girls living in a big house together five minutes from the club. It was very convenient, but very risqué Raven felt. They would occasionally find notes outside the gate telling one of them to give whoever the perpetrator was money. "You got forty-eight hours or else, ladies."

Just dumb shit like that. Though that dumb shit never sat right with Raven though something was always a little off.

"All of you damn well knew how she was the one that hated me, that was jealous of me."

Next day came, and there was a serious news briefing about a missing woman's body being found in the deserted area off of the Fifteen heading toward Los Angeles.

They said a trucker had discovered it, and the body had some severe claw markings across the face down over the chest and sternum to the abdomen. There was some weird symbol carved into her thigh. There was just a think pink piece of clothing hanging off of her.

Raven knew that was Kristen, for they had found her body. "Holy shit," Raven said to herself as she sat up in bed. There was this aching feeling in her loins of just the knowing. Suddenly, the phone rang, and it was Monica, saying, "Did you just see the news briefing? I think they found Kristen's body. I think it was some sort of cult thing because an animal wouldn't and obviously couldn't carve symbols into her skin, and they were postmortem."

Raven said, "Yeah, I did. Just got done watching it too." Suddenly, the phone beeped with a few of the other girls calling in at the same time, it seemed. *This is an absolutely awful thing to happen to anyone*, Raven thought to herself. She then said to Monica on the phone, "I can't even imagine the devastation of her mother, the feeling of that pain." Monica just stayed quiet, except for the sounds of a slight sniffle.

Then the two hung up the phone, which constantly rang on Raven's end at least. She refused to answer, knowing it was some of the other girls from work and couldn't bear it to speak about it any further. She figured she had to get dressed to go into work anyway, so it could wait, if need be.

At work that evening, it was a very somber atmosphere. Even the DJ André wasn't his regular jovial self. When he would announce, "Now coming to the main stage, Minx [Monica]," there was just no feeling in it. It was the same with Blue (Raven). He always kept the girls on their toes and was their biggest fan in the club. With his delicious Bolivian accent and rather handsome self, dark hair, five foot ten, goatee with a faint mustache, there was rumor that he and Kristen were fucking—perhaps because it was also said he was good at everything he did.

Oh well, Raven thought to herself, *not my business*. As Raven approached the back, entering the dressing room, there was a group of girls huddled up, crying. As the housemother stood in the middle and was praying, Monica saw Raven and went running over to her, saying, "Yes, in fact, it was for sure Kristen they found. Her mother went down and identified her remains."

"Wait, what?" Raven said. There was a cluster of freckles behind her right ear, almost covered with her hair that her mom always said looked like Orion's Belt. "Whoa," Raven said, followed by "That's weird but beautiful in a way."

The housemother Hinto came over and said, "Since there were only few areas on her body that weren't ripped up if you will, that was one area kept stayed intact well enough for her to be identified as Kristen Kavowitz." This indeed was a reckoning for them all, as everyone slowly looked around at each other and gave hugs.

Maybe there was something in this situation that would indeed bring the girls closer together and not have so much jealousy and hatefulness brewing on a constant. Would the perpetrator or perpetrators ever be found and brought to justice? Raven didn't know as she thought to herself. She wished there was something she could do. She remembered her Niki and Britany, her rape, and molestation. "Damn," she said. "Where is the silver lining?"

She shook it off as many of the girls tried to do and just focus on going out on the floor to dance. They had to keep surviving in this struggle of life. As the night passed on, it was quiet, calm, and somewhat relaxing. Monica and Raven kind of stayed close to each other throughout that night and the nights that proceeded. One night, they walked into the back of the dressing room after doing a girl-on-girl show together on the stage, where they racked up. They said to each other, "We have been through our stuff, argued, and it got physical only once. Let's make a vow to keep it that way and be close forever." Both of them swore this is what they would do because there was too much evil going on in the world. Suddenly, they heard laughing, you know the kekee, ha type? It was one of the girls, Jenn. She was getting married. Raven and Monica were very excited and happy for her as they group hugged, all jumping up and down together topless in thongs. A man would have loved to walk in on that shit.

So then Monica was like, "We're going to a wedding, Rave."

Jenn just stopped. She stopped smiling and jumping, about saying, "Minx and Blue, you two are not invited though. I'm sorry."

Raven and Monica just looked at each other then looked at Jenn then back at each other, at the same time saying, "What?"

Jenn went to give some bullshit explanation as to why, and the two girls just walked away as if they were sobbing. Then they started laughing, as Jenn turned to look at them in a perplexed manner.

As they walked around the corner to hit the other row where there were lockers, they then looked at each other, all bright-eyed, and said, "Wedding crashers, no wedding crashettes."

Forgive me, Father, for I have sinned.

CHAPTER 14

THE WEDDING CRASHETTES

Raven and Monica did their best to remain close to Jenn and brown-nosed like crazy. Jenn kept saying, "I know you two are going above and beyond to stick by my side just so I can change my mind and invite you to the wedding."

Monica insisted, "No, that's not it at all, Jenn. We just love you dearly."

Raven basically followed it up by saying, "It's just the past event that took place with Kristen still has most of us in an unease state of being." Monica seconded that with a head nod. It seemed as if Jenn understood where Raven was coming from, and she kind of shook her head as well in agreement.

Jenn was an interesting character, very old-fashioned. She adored the pinup look but was a very old-world Hollywood glam like. And she spoke as if from the eighteenth or nineteenth century often.

Like she would say, "Thought I smelt a rat, for aught I know, also agreeance," really outdated old English from the old world. She made it sound sexy though, and that was her thing. The men that came into the club adored her as well and her class. She racked in some big bucks Jenn, very sexy, very thick, a Bridgette Bardot kind of look to her. She wasn't white, wasn't black, and wasn't Spanish. People weren't quite sure what the fuck she was. She had a fairer skin tone. She had that slight gap between her teeth. People, both male and female, wanted her just like they wanted Raven. Plenty of couples would come, asking for a girl-on-girl show of Jenn and Raven.

Jenn had what sounded like a Minnesotan accent or Canadian maybe. Every time they or someone would ask her where she's from, she'd be very secretive and say, "My mother's cunt."

"Whatever the fuck that meant! Just sure it wasn't an old-world style of speaking, so it was rather confusing."

The girls finally found out the whereabouts of Jenn and Marco's wedding and reception party. They would talk secretly among each other about what they were to wear, about if they would just attend the party reception and wedding or just the first. They finally agreed that they would do both. They agreed that they would enter the church, and since it was so vast, they would sit in the back furthest pew, which is the bench-like seating that normally a congregation sits in. In a Catholic church setting, the seating went all the way back, so they knew they'd be well hidden. Then they would leave as the Father said, "You may kiss the bride." They knew at that point all would stand clapping, cheering them on, sobbing the whole fucking works, and that would be their chance to make their exit.

Raven also had realized that the main reason Jenn said they weren't invited was largely due to Marco not wanting them there, well, especially not Monica because she used to fuck Manny, who was Marco's brother, and she went a little crazy on him. She slapped him in public, almost humiliating him in front of some business cohorts when drunk because she's a fucking bitch when she drinks. Being that association brings on assimilation, as they say. That means Raven was cut out for it. Monica shared in detail how she was from Bronx, New York, originally Monica Capellino. She worked in the dance circuit up there while dating an Albanian thug that forced her to be a madame of sorts, making her drive Albanian escorts that were prostitutes around to meet different men. She had only been in Vegas for about two years before she and Raven met. Monica left home at sixteen because she and her mom would always lock horns. Her mother and father later packed up and moved to Paradise, Nevada, right outside of Vegas with little Jimmy.

Monica said, "Yeah, that was my life for a minute. I didn't even have a valid driver's license. He got a fake one for me. Thought that he really owned me and would beat the living shit out of me if I wouldn't drive the girls. Oh, you know shitty with an extra side of shite." Also, it was well known that Monica and Raven became thick as thieves. This crazy stuff Monica went through just brought the two of them closer. It just wouldn't be right to invite one and not the other. The conclusion was neither was to be invited, and that settled that. Marco and Manny were known as the wild boys of Vegas. It seemed like every guy wanted to be them or friends with them. Every girl wanted to fuck them or just be around them alone and close enough to say they did. Marco was smooth and definitely had his way with women. It was just Manny had his way more so. Both were about five feet, ten inches tall, dark, and very handsome with slick black hair and tattoos of various things from snakes to scorpions— the crazy shit but sexy. Manny was a little thicker in stature than his brother Marco, and both walked kind of bowed, like bowleg. Ooh, and Manny, he was quite a character. He was good at getting what he wanted without lifting a finger or spending a dime really. Marco, on the other hand, was very frivolous in his spending habits. That's how I think he courted Jenn in the first place. Oh well, that was history repeating itself in Raven's eyes anyway. It's just that Marco, from what she knew, was exquisitely kind to Jenn. He worshipped the ground she walked upon, as to how it should be.

Their family had gotten their money through some type of oil deal that went rather well. Thusly, when their father died, it was left to them and their sister Marlita. That's why Jenn would always say, "Marco wants me to stop dancing. He wants me to quit."

Raven would just give her advice and tell her, "Make sure he marries you first and have something going on that you could fall back on. For these men say anything at any given time to get what the fuck they want." However, six months had passed on, and the girls waited patiently for this day like no other. The wedding was to be at the Guardian Angel Cathedral on Cathedral Way, Las Vegas, Nevada, a beautiful church built in the early sixties.

They were to be married by the good old Father Vino Chaneli, the pedophile of the Catholic community, so many suspected it. Just no one would really say it but Monica, of course. It was the middle of May, on a gorgeous May spring day.

"It seemed so fitting for a wedding," Raven said to Monica. Then Raven thought, *Damn, finally something wonderful is happening, and even though I wasn't really invited, I get to see it.* The service was for 3:30 p.m. on Saturday. The girls thought they'd show up about 3:15 or 3:20 p.m. *That's ample time for them to get in and get settled without easily being notic*ed, they thought. They also knew Jenn was always late for life.

By that time, they would be sitting, and when to stand as the bride walks down the aisle, they would drop their semi-sheer vails over their hats. That way, no one, not even Jenn, would be none the wiser. They had it all planned out.

The decor was absolutely gorgeous. Jenn wouldn't have it any other way. There were lilies all around with roses of bluish in color. Raven then said, "Wow, and my favorite color, blue. It's like Jenn did the decor for me." Then she smiled so big and bright but had her vail down so one wouldn't be able to see. A few of the wedding guests in the back of the church noticed the two of them enter and go to sit. As they did, there was Father Chaneli walking down the aisle to head up to the front of the church. He looked at them and nodded, and Raven and Monica nodded back then sat.

"Thank heavens Marco didn't notice us," Raven said.

Then Monica said, "Fucking Father Chaneli did, that pedo." Raven nudged Monica to stop and shut up just before they sat. While they were sitting and waiting among everyone else, the organ music began to play.

Father Chaneli said, "Will, everyone, please stand." It was like a domino effect. First, the front area in rows stood and morphed into the back rows and finally to their row. It looked as if it was planned. As the organ music played, here came Jenn as if she was gliding down the aisle, floating really. She was looking absolutely fucking gorgeous, just as the decor in the church setting did. It was something out of an old-world Hollywood glam movie. From her beautiful gown, her hair, even her father, who escorted her down the aisle, looked like a movie star from the forties.

Raven and Monica looked at each other, slightly tearing up. They said to each other, "We just have to get through this boring part of the I dos, and the rest is history." The girls sat as they listened and waited for what seemed like forever.

"Long ass ceremony," Monica leaned in and said to Raven in a modulated voice. "Also, we have to have Father fucking Chaneli give the service."

Raven seconded that with "Yeah, sure is long. As far as Father Vino, he's a man of God, Monica."

Then Monica said, "He's a deviant. I can smell it on him."

Raven just rolled her eyes and listened. They continued to sit, doing their best to sit there peacefully and wait it out then follow the precession to the reception party. That's where the real fun would begin.

Then suddenly, Father Vino said, "You may now kiss your bride."

Everyone stood and clapped. Some people were crying as you pan around the room to look. It was very noticeable. The girls quickly pulled back down their vails. Jenn and Marco were on approach, and also, the rows of pews were unfolding. The formation was on cue for sure.

As their pew they were standing in began unfolding into the rest of the flow, that is where they heard of the venue where the receptions to be held. They waited till the coast was clear enough to slip out the side door. And that was when Monica saw Manny. He had come in to use the restroom right quick before going to join the rest of the groom's men in the limo.

He said to them, "Hello, ladies."

Monica's heart was pumping like she saw a ghost. She just turned her head and looked at him but said nothing as he went on into the men's room.

Raven saw Monica and how she slowed down in a slowed motion way. Monica was a little bit taken aback by the encounter. She then grabbed Monica by the arm, demanding her to snap out of it. "You're literally stuck like Chuck with your finger in your butt. Keep it together." That was one of their things they'd say.

Monica said, "Yeah, yeah, I know, but do you think he recognized us?"

"Who cares? Let's go, Monica. We are on a mission," Raven said.

Marco did kind of slow his pace down while looking at Raven and Monica in what seemed like slow motion, Raven thought to herself. Then they were gone on their way to the Emerald at Queensridge.

It was located in one of the most exclusive communities. It was exquisite—trees, a gazebo on the outside. Inside was a grand staircase with dramatic vaulted ceilings. The decor in the ballroom was a complete old-Hollywood style. It was really a dream come true for a girl. Well, once they arrived there, there were already a good number of guests present, so they just slid right in.

Of course, Monica headed straight to the bar to order a cocktail. Raven warned her, "Don't let yourself drink too fucking much, woman, for you might forget where we are and show her ass too much." She meant this both figuratively and literally.

Things were going nicely, very smoothly. They drank, danced, ate very little of the food although it was delicious, you know, figures and all. Raven told Monica she would be right back. She had to use the ladies' room.

Monica, all alone standing there, felt a tap on her shoulder. She then took a deep breath, not turning around immediately, for she knew that touch. It was Manny. He was the only one that could give her that feeling of knowing you're alive, but you're not breathing for what seems like an eternity, but you know you're still alive…how?

Suddenly, she then said to herself three times in a row, "Get it together. Keep it together, Monica."

Suddenly, she turned around with vail down on her hat and said, "Hello," in some ridiculous British accent.

Manny, looking a little bewildered, said, "I…I apologize. I must have thought."

That's when Raven was making her way over and noticed. Then Monica said, "No need," as she walked off toward Raven.

"Whew, that was close," Monica said. Manny stood in the background, just glaring toward their direction, watching every move they made.

Raven then said, "Damn it, Monica, what did you say to him? He can't seem to take his eyes off of you."

Monica said, "All I did was say hello, then no need."

Raven turned her lip up, just looking at Monica. For she knew Monica and knew there was more to the story than that. Monica finally admitted she put on her ridiculous British accent. Raven was like, "I knew it, I knew it, can't leave your crazy ass alone for one fucking minute, Monica."

Monica was holding a glass in her hand and then suddenly placed it abruptly on a nearby cocktail tray a server was carrying and said, "I'll be right back."

Raven was like, "Wait a minute, where are you going?"

Monica then said, "To the restroom, Raven. You can come if you want."

Raven thought to herself, *Hell, I better go. There is no telling what this girl is going to get into or say to anyone at any given second, especially with drinks in her.* They both made a B-line for the restroom, Monica walking very swiftly. They passed the ladies, and Raven said, "Mon, wait, slow down. The women's is right—"

Before he could even get the word here out, Monica slammed open the men's restroom door and approached Father Chaneli, grabbing him by his little sink ass nuts and said, "I know you and know what you did, and soon the world will know what you are."

Father Chaneli then said, "Excuse me, this is preposterous. What in the heavens are you talking about, lady, and this is the men's restroom?"

Monica said, "Hey, Ra, lock the door. Lock the fucking door, please."

Raven, shaking some, just locked it and stood there, watching.

Monica then went on to say, "Remember little Jimmy, the one you would call my little Jimmy? Well, that's my little Jimmy, my little fucking brother, you piece of shit. I know what you did to him."

Father Chaneli then began to say, "What? I have no idea what you speak of, young lady. I am a Father, a well-respected priest here and abroad."

Monica interrupted, saying, "Lies all lies. You're a fucking liar. Liar is what you are, a disgusting liar that preys on young boys, hiding behind God and your fucking church. You use God as a cloak to hide your darkness, and this is real. I hate you and everything you stand for." Then she spit in his face, following by saying, "My little brother blew his fucking head off because of what you did. You are a fucking liar. All you do is lie, and the truth will come out one day!" Monica screamed this at him.

It got kind of frightening in that bathroom. Raven really thought that Monica was to off Father Vino right there. Monica just kept yelling all these obscenities to him as Raven stood there in shock with her lips trembling.

Monica then released Father Chineli's genitals and whispered in his ear, "Repent for the power of Christ is compelling." Then she slapped the shit out of him, turned toward the door, unlocked it. Then she and Raven walked out.

As they both looked at each other, deciding maybe it was time to leave, Raven was like, "What in the hell was that just in the men's room, and why did you not tell me this, Monica?"

Monica told Raven, "It isn't something you just share."

Raven was like, "Mon, I am so sorry. I get it, well sort of now I know why there has been so much coldness in you." It seemed as if many would always try to placate Monica. Raven saw this quite often. She finally fully understood why Monica had her moments. It was little Jimmy, Monica's brother, who blew his fucking head off with a shotgun, that was weighing on her. She then hugged Monica, holding her tight, saying, "I love you, girl, and I am here for you."

Monica just brushed it off, pushing Raven back slightly, saying, "Yeah, I know, and thanks but makeup."

That was Monica, Raven thought and just scoffed. Then she said, "Let's go."

Suddenly, here came Manny walking over, saying, "Hello, Monica, it is a pleasure to see you here. I am not sure because last I heard, you weren't invited, although you do look stunning."

Monica held her head up high and looked at Manny, saying, "Thank you. You look pretty handsome yourself."

As Raven began to speak to say how they were not invited, Manny interjected and said, "May I have this dance?" Monica, speechless, gave him her hand in acceptance. He said hello to Raven while she just stood aside in awe, not trying to say anything else as he took Monica to the dance floor.

Manny pulled Monica in close, and they danced, laughing, talking like they were a couple again. It was actually really refreshing looking at the two of them, Raven thought.

Manny had said to Monica in her ear, "Don't worry, I already explained to my brother and his new wife that I invited you two to come, so just relax."

Monica was like, "Hmm, I knew it."

The two headed over to the bar to get a drink, and Raven came, walking up while Monica all smiles from ear to ear said, "It's all right, Rave. Jean and Marco know we are here. Manny told them earlier that he had invited us and would take full responsibility, so we are not wedding crashettes anymore, Rave."

As relieving to Raven as this was, Raven then said, "No, we just hold people hostage and assault them." At the same token though, Raven did understand.

"It was nothing to do with you, Raven, the recent bathroom episode," Monica said. Apparently, it was a green light for all crazy things because well, Monica knew Manny knew they were at the function. Manny then turned to the ladies, giving Raven a glass of champagne and then one to Monica, and the three stood and saluted. "Wedding crashettes, Monica?" Manny said. While laughing, Manny said, "Thought it was wedding crashers? I see the twist there, and I like it, so here's to two sexiest ass women at the wedding reception, the sedding crashettes. Salud."

Then Monica pulled Manny in close and took his hand as she pulled up part of her gown and placed it between her legs. All seemed well like it was okay like everything was really okay. Raven rolled her eyes then smiled, thinking Monica needs this moment to get her mind off of the earlier episode with Father Vino, and she went, walking off to go outside and see the grounds and smoke a joint she was holding for Monica. "Why not?" she said.

As she approached the gazebo, lighting the joint and taking some hits, she saw the chiffon ribbons blowing in the light breeze in the night. She then saw Father Chaneli with his hand up on one of the columns outside there. He was kinda swaying back and forth. She just said to herself, "I know he isn't drunk. He doesn't drink. I don't think. He's a priest, but who knows. Monica can make anyone lose their fucking shit. I mean, anything is possible after Hurricane Monica." She then saw a hot-ass woman in an ivory-colored cream fitted gown with an umbrella with gold trimming. Raven tried to be flush with the column so she would not be seen. The woman was shaking her hand in his face, pointing. She then pulled out some paper, holding it in front of Father Chaneli. She turned and walked off after slapping his face as well. "Is this 'who can slap Father Vino' night? I mean, what the fuck is going on?" Raven said. She remained hidden and slowly emerging to see what she could see.

Then she saw him take a step back with his dick hanging out of his pants. He tucked it in and zipped it up. She ducked down because she didn't want to be seen that she saw this. The entire time, she was saying, "If Monica saw this, what the fuck would she do? She probably would confront him again and worse because of her deep dislike for Father Chaneli, and she didn't care who knew it." He then walked off by himself, then she came out and sat down, exhaling and was somewhat relieved. She then said, "You see, Monica, Father Vino is a man of God, still a man probably taking a leak outside like all men do." Just as she did, she saw one of the younger altar boys running off through the bushes. Her mouth fell open, and she dropped the joint and just looked at it and said, "Damn, this shit is potent weed." She then said, "Holy shit." If shit was indeed holy, now was the time for it. "Monica was right and poor little Jimmy. Holy shit, Father fucking Vino Chaneli."

Do we put more faith in the ones that say they are a servant of the Lord?

CHAPTER 15

FATHER FUCKIN' VINO CHANELI

Father Chaneli was a tall, prominent figure of Italian descent from Rome, Italy itself. In the city of Vegas, everyone knew and adored him a little too much because parents would allow their young children to be around him at all times and be at his summer camp with their permission. Young boys were so enamored with Father Vino. They would throw fits to be able to go and be part of his summer camp year after year.

There was so much talk in the community of him being a pedophile though. Going back to Italy, it came out that there were decades of attempts by the Catholic church to cover up incidents involving him and priests.

Guess that is why he came to the States. He's Father Vino. He would never, and he could never. Well, that's where many were wrong.

He'd been a priest in the community for almost two decades already. Well, the day finally came that a young man, now twenty years in age, came forth, stating that he had sexual relations with Father Vino on numerous occasions in the church rectory. He said that Father Vino promised him his love only and that they would be with him forever if he would lure other young boys into the rectory so he could videotape them having sex and orgies.

This went on since the young man was nine years of age. Father Vino would organize scout summer camps for the boys in the community, and it was okay because he was Father Vino, loved and respected by all. This is how he got away with molesting these young boys for so long. And little Jimmy was one that was part of this summer camp porn for boys it came out. Shortly after these allegations were made against Father Vino, the rectory at the church was set on fire. The perpetrator, another young man bout seventeen or so, came forth, stating that he and Father Chaneli were supposed to move in together once he became of age to move out. He said he torched the rectory because he was trying to hide the evidence of the sexually deviant acts that occurred inside and realized it was wrong. There were hundreds of tapes, the boy said. He admitted to being in at least 120 of them himself. Unfortunately, not all were destroyed, and even with Father Vino being arrested and kicked out as top clergy member due to the allegations themselves, the tapes had him dead to rights. Even with that, he was still defiant and dismissive.

In Father Vino's room, there were over two hundred hours of homemade sex tapes alone. Crazy how most were made in the rectory right under the noses of other priests there. Young boys dressed in leather and bondage, and some boys were asked to convince their own brothers into sexual relations and the mothers. Little Jimmy walked in on Father Chaneli, beating a boy with the help of his main lover to death. They then threatened little Jimmy and his family to him. Father Vino Chaneli then demanded that Jimmy help them dispose of the remains of the boy they killed. "So this and I am sure other reasons from this world is why little Jimmy blew his own fucking head off at fourteen years old," Raven said to herself while having the thought of damn she saw him that night of Jenn and Marco's wedding outside of the reception at the Emerald Queensridge played back in her mind. It was obscene with him definitely getting his nasty dick sucked by a young altar boy—all these thoughts and talk of this and Monica always knowing there was something up with his nasty perverted ass. She'd always say, "That motherfucker tries to act like a man of God, hiding under the cloak of the blood of Jesus. He's a bigger sinner than all of us put together. I will bet my life on it."

Monica was absolutely right, it seemed. Then more and more young boys to young men came forth, telling of the damnation they suffered at the hands of Father Vino. Some said he would force them to smoke hashish and drink whiskey because God said the ride would be smoother with the intake of drugs and liquor. Father Vino's definition of the ride was having these young boys mount him and take him inside of them into, well, you know, especially after he would insert a barbiturate into their rectums. His abuse resonated deeply throughout a lot of them.

As Raven discovered more and more of these events, she threw up. One even presented a lawsuit against him and the entire clergy, winning an undisclosed amount. The evidence was irrefutable with no way of getting out or around this. "How are they even allowed in this world we live in?" Then she thought about previous things in her life that occurred, and it saddened her. This made her realize it happened and could happen to anyone, girl, boy, woman, or man. One of the security/bouncers at the club approached Father Chaneli coming down the courthouse steps. He drew his gun and shot Father Vino six times in the genitals. When they apprehended him, he said, "That was for my nephew Jordan."

Wow, Raven thought, *that's very close to home.* She started having reservations about her life there and all the recent events. These events were causing her to remember dark times, especially times she hid away from in her mind.

She then decided she didn't want to dance anymore and talked to Monica about moving away to Colorado or California or something to become a women's rights activist, people's rights activist. She would give herself a year and make as much as she could. She said, "Jenn has stopped. We can too. We don't have to get married to be able to do so."

She only had a few friends that she worked with in the club. O was in and out, mostly out because she was now living with her rapper boyfriend in California. Unfortunately, Raven did not hear from O that much. It didn't help that O's man did not like Raven too much because she would not allow him to wrap her around his finger. The other friends, well, one was an alcoholic sometimes, who was Monica, and one played the alcoholic all the time, and on a drug binge, she would do her shit but handle it, who was Cindy—leaving one to be a functioning alcoholic, all the time crashing cars into mailboxes and her own garage door, who was Kimber.

CHAPTER 16

SHIVER ME, KIMBER

Shiver me, Kimber, that's how Andre, the DJ at the club, would announce her to be presented to the stage to perform. In her little schoolgirl outfit, perfect plaid skirt, white shirt, and white knee-high socks. Let's pay homage to Britany Spears's "Baby Hit Me One More Time." She looked like a Selma Hayek. For some reason, she would get such an evil look on her face when she would be drunk. But guess what, the guys loved it. She would literally walk up to some of them and place the point of her stiletto heel in their crouch and tell them they are going to dance with her. I'll be damned if it didn't work every time. Both Monica and Kimber could throw down some vodka like nobody's damn business.

As far as Kimber, *forget* about it, the cake was taken there. They were all guilty of drunk driving. The only thing was Monica never got caught doing so. And now that Kristen was gone, Andre had his eye on Kimber. It was a busy Saturday night in the club. It was packed wall to wall with patrons of both males and females.

Dances were just flowing like water, which was a great thing. Andre had the music, bumping good songs. He even played in between the girls dancing their set on stage. The line to the private room was down the stairs. Kimber was dancing for a dude back to back then. When she got down off the stage, she encountered a couple that wanted her to dance, but she had to do another stage set first. They both then sat around the stage and waited for her, tipping her constantly with each move she made.

She would do this thing where she bent over and touched her toes, grabbing her ankles where her pussy lips would puff up, and you could see it through her thong, very sexy because she would get a little wet, and it would make her thong more translucent. That night in particular, as she danced her set on the stage, there was a greasy foreign-looking guy that she was dancing in front of and doing this, doing that. He wouldn't give her a dollar, not that he didn't have. He just wouldn't. Until the chic with the guy said to him, "Tip her! Damn it. She's hot and doing all this shit." Then there were a group of thugs right there on the other side, saying, "Yeah, come bring that fat ass pussy over here and drop with it." Kimber would talk shit to these motherfuckers. She did not give a fuck. They were known bangers too.

Back to the fucking greaseball, not giving her anything. It's like he was in a trance, not blinking or anything. He did tip her finally though after one of the thug-like niggas put him a choke hold then took the rest of his cash after what looked like no less than a hundred-dollar bill he gave her.

Kimber then went to the pole and climbed it slowly and spun around it, doing tricks. Then slowly, she slid down on it, rubbing her pussy lips on the pole while they were all puffed out. People started screaming and cheering her on. "Yeah, baby" was screamed a couple of times.

Then one guy said, "That pussy is pumping just for me." Kimber heard him and made her way over to him, dancing on stage right next to him but more so for another guy to see. She loved teasing the fuck out of the guys that came in there, especially the loud, obnoxious ones. As she was dancing, the rude guy reached over and rubbed his fingertips over her pussy lips, and before he could finish, she did some twisty move. She had her heel in his mouth like he was sucking her heel like a dick. She then proceeded to kick him clearly in the face with her other foot using the ball of her foot while "Down with the Sickness" by Disturbed was blaring in the background. He then went flying off the stool, smack dead in the ground. The thug niggas were like, "Damn, Ma, you a mess." Andre also saw it and was over there, quick fast in a hurry, for he was very skilled in combat fighting. By that time, security had grabbed the guy literally by the nostrils, dragging him out the back door of the club.

That was Kimber, and that was Andre. They didn't give a shit. They fucked people up and maybe asked questions later. Plus, the thugs were Andre's boys, and that is why they could get away with shit in the club. Andre's gang he kicked it with were cool with them—like some sort of big gangster family. Kimber's brother was also part of another Latino gang in Honduras with some big connections in Vegas. It was all intertwined. Andre did have a sick MMA skill set, which started from his gang affiliations. Unfortunately, Andre did not fight anymore with the MMA after getting kicked out for some heavy fucking criminal shit, he said. So his coach talked with him and said he'd rather not report him because he would face some serious time. Therefore, he took the lesser of the two evils.

Kimber's brother Danito was very close to Andre. He was the real crazy one though. Once, her brother was bitten by a stray dog in Honduras. He got very angry about it. He then went home, cooked three entire chicken with the most delicious fragrant of spices, got a bunch of glass bottles, crushed them up, stuffed the bird with the fine broken, crushed glass, and coated the outside of it with the fine glass and spices. Danito then took the chicken out and put it in the middle of the street, knowing all the strays would come from everywhere ravaging this cooked chicken.

Shortly after that, dogs were found dead on the streets over in Honduras, block after block of dead dogs. He felt like that was his payback for the one dog biting him.

Somehow with all her brother's connections, she felt like she was allowed to do whatever she wanted. One night, in fact, she was drunk driving. She ran her car through her own garage door, as said earlier, damaging a brand-new washer and dryer set still in the boxes. Someone came over, banging on the door, and when Kimber opened it, they said, "Someone just drove a car through your garage door, is everything—"

Before they could finish, Kimber then said, "I know, bitch. It was me. Now get off my fucking doorstep and leave me the fuck alone."

She didn't give a fuck and would cuss your ass out in a heartbeat.

In any event, after her set was over, she went to go dance for the couple that was waiting patiently for her to get off the stage. Well, they were just friends coming there to have a good time. Kimber sat and had a drink with them. Then came a shot then another. She then danced for each one of them a couple of times.

They wanted to go to the private room with her, so the three of them did. And she was dancing for him then dancing for the female and putting her hands on her tits, telling her she would get friendly with her more and more depending on how long they stay. She put her tits in her face then placed her nipple in her mouth as she gently sucked it. Then the guy there was like, "Wait a minute, I didn't get to suck it." Men, they get so whiny like little ass bitchy children, you know.

Then the female patron was like, "All right, he's getting a little bit baby-like over there. Please go and give him some attention." She then danced, keeping it sexy still song after song, just barely touching his lips with her nipples as she put them across his face. His female companion looked down at his dick and could see him bulging in his pants. Kimber saw it too and sat on it while she looked deep in her eyes.

She sat on his hard rail like did and began to lap dance him, going in harder and more intense each song that played. As she danced and guided on it, she could feel him throbbing. Then he stopped and grabbed her hips to hold her down on his lap because he didn't want to cum. He said, "Don't move. Please don't move. I am trying not to cum." Kimber loved that shit and did not care. She loved the power that she would have over the men that came into the club. Kimber lifted herself up, turned around to face him, then straddled him. And she started hard grinding and grinding. She then got up and could see his jeans were soaking through as he was convulsing from orgasm.

Then his companion said, "Ooh, look at you. You just got fucked hard." Kimber was known for making men cum in their pants, most of the time with just her foot. He then had the biggest smile on his face while getting up to use the men's room to clean up as best he could from that sexisode of dance. As he returned, he walked up on Kimber and his companion in a deep intense lip-lock of a kiss. He just watched and waited patiently until they were through. Then he sat back down on the couch next to them both. He suddenly looked up and saw one of the other strippers walk past in what seemed like a drugged-up stupor. She actually approached the three of them sitting there and said something that was some type of gobbledygook then walked off.

The guy was like, "What the hell was that?"

Kimber just laughed and announced, "We call her Bingy Cindy because she always looks like she's on some type of drugged-out binge. It's crazy. She's cool though. We're actually friends."

At the same time, both the chic and the guy went, "Oh, got it. The name is fitting."

They all three headed up front to wrap up on the credit card because the charges came to more than he had cash available on hand. They paid Kimber out for all three hours and extra in cash on top then said, "Thank you. We had a great time."

Kimber followed with "You're welcome. Thanks for coming in, guys. Later."

Kimber then went to the back as all the girls do in the club to get freshened up, eat, count their cash, etc. Then on the floor in the shower area, there was Bingy Cindy.

CHAPTER 17

BINGY CINDY

That chic was really "throwed," a slang used from an urban stand-point when someone is really fucked in the head from drugs and alcohol or just because they're straight fucked genetically maybe. Cindy was always on a binge of getting fucked up, hence the name Bingy Cindy. It's like people thought Kristen was seriously fucked up. Nope. Cindy took the cake, so you would think. The truth with Cindy is she would fake it. Well, she'd be on shit but handle it like a rock star, played the whole game off as if she was extra fucked up. Somehow, this bitch could turn it off and on, snap in and out of that shit like a pro. She would just put it all out there like it was nothing. She would try to have conversations with you, and to her, she was fully cognizant of what was going on, but others had no fucking clue on either end of the spectrum, even the girls in the club that she befriended, except for Raven—she knew the game. Perhaps she got far because the guys thought she was just Dingy Cindy, if you will. Not to mention she was very, very pretty even when "supposedly fucked up."

How in the hell did she pull that shit off? Everyone wondered how in the hell, Cindy, hot, blond, not hot because she's blond, blond, just fucking hot. She was a dreamy-looking woman, five foot ten, supermodel physique, sweet as all hell, strange though, big blue eyes like an anime character. She wore her hair in bangs but long. She had an average breast size, but her vagina lips looked like a pork chop. This was discovered when a few of the girls went skinny-dipping and saw that Cindy's lips were literally floating like a water-logged pork chop. It was weird but funny ass shit to be seen. Even when she wore her thong at the club, it was so meaty down there and thick. She made a grip of money in the club on going. Her thing was she would wet her whistle with vodka and then whatever it was the guy she was giving attention to that evening liked. She would tip the bartender or server a little extra to make her shots watered down with a splash of vodka. Or if they were sitting at the bar and the guy was looking directly to see what the bartender was pouring, she would take the shot in the hand and just act dingy and laugh till the bartender came over. Then once that occurred, they would be a little bit distracted. She'd laughed again and grab his leg while wetting her lips with the vodka then tossing the rest somehow quickly. They never saw a thing. It was actually brilliant.

Cindy actually had a degree in psychology, a bachelor's, she said. She was thirty-three but looked like she was maybe nineteen. She was a single mother who had a son named Connor by a meth-head father that had disappeared running off with some meth-head junkie chic. Misery likes company, it is said. In any event, Connor was kicked out of the fourth grade for sniffing another child's bicycle seat. Connor was caught outside more than once doing this. The little girl whose bicycle it was was named Candace.

Connor said, "Candace smells like candy. I like candy, so I sniff and lick her bicycle seat."

The school contacted Cindy right away and told her, "He's ten years old. Where does he get this from?"

Cindy said, "Exactly only ten and you want to expel him?"

Connor was very bright, more so than the other children in his class. I guess he'd get bored easily, maybe because he wasn't challenged enough academically. However, of course, Cindy had to make an appearance at the school and plead her argument. Raven went with her in tow, even witnessing on Connor's behalf. Unfortunately, nothing positive came of it, for Connor was a mess, much like his mom and always challenging teachers or other staff at school. Perhaps the combination of all was too much for the facility to further handle, so removal was the only option. He was just very intelligent, maybe a little too much that it worked against him. He just did dumb shit for attention, like sniffing and licking his classmate's bicycle seat.

Cindy would be all right, for sure. She would soon get Connor into another school where the curriculum was even better, and they were more patient and understanding of a child's needs. So that she did immediately and was a better mother for it. She even decided to go out on a date with a guy she met, drove out to him in California, and didn't tell any of her friends of the address.

That did shit like that on a whim that was Cindy. Good thing she did these things when she was mostly sober. This time around, she thought she was going to die.

She went on a date with this Rudy. They went walking on the beach after having a drink at his place nearby. There was an inlet from the main part to the beach sand area. On the way back through to his truck, Cindy was walking and starting to feel hot by her ankles then up between her legs. She started thinking to herself, *What the fuck is going on?*

She went and got to his truck after he opened the door for her. As she was sitting there, she could feel her face swelling and throat closing up, followed by some intense pain all over but especially down by her feet and ankles with perfuse itching in her vaginal area. They arrived back at his place, and she went upstairs with him and started to try to hide her face. She went to the bathroom and saw herself contorting right before her own eyes. Her face was swelling up in a lumpy format by the second. "What the fuck?" she said.

She was trying to cover her face with her hair as best as possible because she really liked this hot ass guy chiseled from stone pretty much. She headed back out to the bedroom, and he started to kiss her, and her breath was literally being taken away from her, not from the kisses, not at all. It was from her going into anaphylactic shock from something that bit her maybe. She was all alone out there just with this guy she had recently met. She thought she was going to die, and he was going to throw her body in the back of his pickup truck. "Oh my god, I am all alone here truly, and nobody knows my whereabouts."

Also, knowing about Oliviette and her dealings with her ex that sent an entity to her was freaking her out. Everybody knew about that crazy shit. Weird stuff would happen back in the locker/dressing room of the club, and people would think it was that fucking Kervan guy. As she was looking at herself in the mirror in the bathroom, her mind started playing tricks on her. She started to visualize what she thought was someone or thing behind her. Cindy said, "Please, I know Oliviette. She's not a close friend though. I'm going to die. I'm going to die," thinking could it even be possible for this entity to even come to Cindy, to latch onto her. Why? That made her hyperventilate even worse.

She calmed down some and realized she had to have eaten something or gotten bit by something. Then she decided to tell him, "I am having a bad reaction to something that I think bit me or something at or near the beach."

He followed her in the bathroom while she was still trying to hide her face from embarrassment. He moved her hair and said, "It's going to be all right. Let me see." By this time, he was asking her questions, and she couldn't talk anymore. Her throat had closed upon her.

He gave her a Benadryl. Being he was in the military, he knew some of what to do, he told her. He gave her a glass of water to drink, and it felt like she was swallowing rocks. It's crazy how your throat can close up that quickly.

Still in panic mode, she kept looking at herself in the mirror, turning into a creature. There was talk of an elephant-woman real-life existence. Ever heard of her?

She was real, and Cindy thought for sure she was turning into her. "Stop panicking, Cindy," she said to herself. She then came back out of the bathroom, still trying to hide her face from this gorgeous man she was with. She started to realize that he was of no threat to harming her. If anything, he was trying to save her.

He grabbed her, holding her close, and just cuddled her in his arms. Whatever it was he was doing, it was soothing her and calming her down.

It actually helped her to fall asleep in his arms. When she awoke, her face was almost normal. Her vagina was no longer hot, not from being bitten anyway. Her throat was opened again, but her feet were still swollen, and one was somewhat numb. He asked her, "How are you feeling?"

She responded, "I feel better for the most part."

He said, "I think you got bitten by fire ants. They're very prevalent in these parts of southern California."

"Oh shit, really?"

He then pulled her in close, this time kissing her, then her neck, her breasts down to her pussy and eating it like a delicacy. He put on a condom and slowly slipped it in, fucking her good, passionately, a little slow then a little fast. She had some of the most intense orgasms ever to be felt. It was so good, back-to-back squirting all over like a hydrant.

This man, Rudy, was just the right getaway for Cindy. He was absolutely fucking gorgeous. He was close to six feet tall, bald head, green eyes, body like a Greek god, and delicious, and he ate her pussy like a champ devouring a delicacy, a pork chop delicacy, not to mention how he fucked her body like never before. She did not want to have feels for this man, but the way he cuddled her, cared for her, and fucked her made her feel like no other.

They fell asleep together again in peaceful silence. It was such a great moment of delicious ecstasy for Cindy that she relished in and wanted to share her excitement.

The next day, she was out having lunch with Jarred and his Eurocentric friend from Scotland, who came walking up wearing a kilt. She swallowed deeply because you could see the outline of his dick. Let's just say he left nothing to be desired this Scotsman. Oh, how she longed for one or some of her girls to be there with her just to see this encounter of the Scotsman, oh boy.

A clootie for your dumplin'

CHAPTER 18

THE SCOTSMAN

This Scotsman had an interesting character. He would actually introduce himself as such. He was tall, at least six foot five, spiky black hair, Asian-shaped blue eyes with a high ass and thick legs. He was a businessman of some sort and distributed liquor. He owned a couple of high-class nightclubs on Sunset and Hollywood Boulevard in Los Angeles. He did love women but also sheep and men. "What?" Exactly. That was his thing, perverse eccentrics. Little did Cindy know or her friends that were about to have the most out of left field encounter with this Scotsman. Loclan, the Scotsman, Loc for short, did it all or definitely wanted to do. He was very respectful and kind and loved to wine and dine.

Raven and Monica got wind of Cindy, and her adventure took off to California. Cindy finally touched base with them and invited them out and told them to grab Matty and to take him with. Matty was the girl's eccentric gay friend. He was the best. They all adored the shit out of Matty. "However, when you come out, especially you, Raven, you may want to stay a while since you talked of moving over here."

Raven was all for it because she had wanted to go to California to see O anyway since she moved, not to mention eventually move out there. So the two of them cussed Cindy out on the phone because she had been gone already a week and a half. Given all the crazy things that had taken place and the crazies in the world, they were in their right.

In any event, Cindy was able to assuage them both and little effort in persuading them to come out and join. Matty was already out in California for some LGBTQ events. They forgot he told them about previously. Raven and all they weren't worried about though because they were sure they'd run into him at some point. They all hung out at one of the Scotsman's lounge spots. Monica was already sitting down inside, chatting up with Cindy when the Scotsman approached.

Cindy introduced Monica, then the Scotsman's attention got diverted the second as he saw Raven coming from the ladies' room and then said, "Nice to meet you, Monica, but will you ladies excuse me a second." He nodded as he walked off, watching Raven as she bent down to fix the strap of her heel. He loved her legs, and it drew him in. He made his way to her, asking if everything was all right.

Raven looked up and smiled softly, saying, "Yes, I am fine. Thank you." He then reached out his hand to grab hers to court her so to say. She put her hand in his. Then he introduced himself as Loclan. Then she said her name was Raven. They chatted it up a minute or two. Then he escorted her over to Monica and Cindy.

"So these are your friends, yes?"

She continued to smile and said, "Yes."

Cindy said, "Well, I guess there is no need for me to make an introduction anymore. You two seemed to have met and hit it off already." Raven looked at Cindy in a perplexing manner.

Cindy then said, "This is the Scotsman Raven."

He then half smiled, nodding his head from side to side, "Scotsman, yes, this is my nickname given my Scottish heritage and all, but my birth name is Loclan."

Raven said, "Oh, I get it. I was a little lost for a minute there." She then started to laugh, and they all joined in laughing with her.

Loclan seemed so intrigued with the likeness of Raven and could not stop staring at her legs. They stayed and talked and talked for what seemed like hours.

He invited her back to his place, and she went where they talked some more, and he offered her some thirty-year-old brandy that he made. She tried it and thought it to be delicious. He then kissed her and asked her to stay. She declined his offer but accepted his offer to go to dinner later in the week.

Later in the week came, and he took her to a French restaurant that had a very quaint setting and was kind of hidden in the Hollywood Hills area.

"The French onion soup is delicious," she said. They had a great time talking and eating, seeing a couple of celebrities come in and out high as kites. Some of which were just staring at her.

That's Hollywood, she thought.

Loc said, "Let's go back to my place and enjoy each other over some of my fine liquor."

Raven went in hand as he courted her out of the restaurant to his home.

She went in upstairs. They sat on the couch, talked, laughed, and drank. They made out on the couch heavily. He then whispered in her ear, "I want to show you something, so keep your eyes closed until I tell you to open them."

Raven said, "Okay, I will."

The Scotsman went into his bedroom, got a blindfold, and put it over Raven's eyes. He then went back to his bedroom for about five to ten minutes. He then came back into the living area where he left Raven sitting and came up close to her, grabbing her hands and putting them on this shotgun he came out with. She remained calm even though she knew what it was but could not see. He then took her hand and placed it on his thigh.

She could feel something lacelike up high. She took a deep breath, still remaining calm. The Scotsman started fingering her, and she got so turned on. He then removed her blindfold, and she saw him dressed in red lingerie, wearing a leather pig's face like a mask with platform red pumps.

"What is this all about?" she said to herself. "This indeed is one for the books," although she had no idea of what was to come next.

He escorted her to his bedroom. Raven's heart was beating like crazy. She didn't know if it was from the liquor, the fingering, the wondering of what's next, or all the above. He then started fucking her slow but hard, and she came very powerfully squirting at times, then he came too. Loc then got up, went to his closet, pulled out a huge black strap on cock. He stood her up and told her, "I want you to wear this." He strapped it on her and said, "Now you are going to fuck me with my Big Black," as he called it.

Raven, at this point, was like, "Holy shit! This is happening. I am about to fuck this manly looking man in the ass with a huge strap on."

The Scotsman wasted no time in getting down. He then bent over and pulled her close, telling her, "Put it in my ass. Fuck my ass like you want to have your way with me, Raven."

She inserted Big Black up in the Scotsman ass and proceeded to fuck him and fuck him good. He was taking it like a champ, she thought. He then pulled away and sat on it, bouncing up and down like a wild ass bitch, jerking at his dick at the same time, then actually screamed as he came hard and a lot.

He lifted himself off of the strap-on and said, "Thank you, my dear. That was amazing." Raven just sat there, staring at the Scotsman, and he said, "Honey, don't be in shock. These are some of the fun, exciting things that life has to offer."

She quickly snapped out of it and went to take a shower then leave as he asked her to please stay the night. She did, and he held her close, and they actually had sex again in the late hours of the night. Then morning came, and he made her breakfast in bed. They talked about him being from Scotland and not in the States that long, giving the thick accent. Raven thought he had a strong sex appeal to him in which he did. He was definitely a different breed of man in so many ways. She then said, "I really have to go, Loc. I mean, my friends do want to spend some time together."

The Scotsman was like, "Raven, why don't you and Monica come over later or even tomorrow because I know that Jarred has some plans for Cindy to go to a winery up north."

Raven said, "Well, we will see what Monica wants to do."

The girls hung out, had lunch that day, and Raven told them about her sexisode with the Scotsman, and both the girls' mouths fell open. I mean, who would not.

"Yes, women do talk too. Women love to share with girlfriends their sexual exploits in life as much as men," Raven said very brashly.

Monica chimed in, saying, "Fuckin' right. I like it."

They all laughed until Raven only said, "Monica, by the way, the Scotsman asked if you wanted to come for dinner and drinks?"

Before Raven could even finish, Monica stopped laughing then took a sip of her tea and nearly spit it through her nose.

Then Raven said, "Are you okay? I didn't mean like that. What I meant was since Cindy is going up to wine country with Rudy, I mean, why not, right?"

Monica sat and gave it some thought then agreed. "Of course," she said. "Yeah, why not?"

Once again, they all chuckled, laughing, taking it all in. They all three went out that night, a ladies' night out on the town if you will.

Raven all donned in her blue, of course. It was her favorite color, remember? Monica was in her pink. The girl loved her pink. Cindy, in black, loved to be a little vixen like.

They partied up the night, dancing it away, reminiscing of other times, even cheering to Kristen, which was a good thing. As they gathered on the dance floor of a nearby nightclub, they encountered a young man by the name of Christopher.

This guy was something from somewhere with long hair, slight body wave texture, dark sultry eyes. Was it kind of an interview with the vampire-looking-like look?

With full sexy lips and very well-spoken and extremely intel-lectual, Monica quickly penned him Long Hair Don't Care, LHDC. She whispered in Raven's ear, "He is LHDC, Long Hair Don't Care, and he looks like he'd eat such good pussy. My inner thigh is wet from my drip." Monica loved to wear her little skirts and no panties, fearful the line would show.

Raven just stepped back and looked at Monica in a perplexed way. Then Monica said, "What?" looking at Raven then at Cindy as they eyeballed her down. Monica then said, "I don't know, but he is turning me on. Why do you girls get to have all the fun?" She also said, "Technically, I am single, and I think I want to fuck him. He's different."

Raven and Cindy just looked at each other, shrugged their shoulders, and said, "Okay," in unison, it seemed.

He bought them drinks and spent damn near the entire night with them while they were out, thoroughly enjoying all three of their company but most especially taking a big liking to Monica, who was fucking wasted at this point in the game. Very wasted, she wanted to leave and did all right. As soon as she hit the corner from the nightclub, she began to take off her clothes, wasn't wearing a lot. She became completely naked as Raven and Cindy were screaming at her. She made an abrupt turn onto Santa Monica Boulevard, streaking all the way and strutting, showing her nakedness!

That Monica, so free-spirited, just wild, which would cause her to get into the troubles that she has and possibly will, Raven thought to herself. She definitely adored Monica.

So did this Long Hair Don't Care character. Completely smitten with Monica, he ran up behind her, scooping her up in his arms quickly, spinning her around. Then they stopped. She was laughing, and they started kissing. This all in the middle of Santa Monica. My gosh, it was a sight as cars passing by beeping, some yelling, "Get the fuck out of the middle of the boulevard, you dumb asses."

They did not care, no fazing for them. Long Hair Don't Care, Christopher, was wearing two shirts. Thank the heavens for that because he removed the top one and placed it on Monica as she just giggled, turning suddenly shy. Where there was no shy bone that existed in this petite girl's body, suddenly, it seemed as that was all she was made up of.

Good times, good times. We all ended the night back at the hotel they were staying at. Next day, Raven awoke to Monica and Christopher fucking the hell out of each other up against the hotel window.

Christopher wanted Raven to watch and whispered in Monica's ear, "Tell her to watch." He loved voyeurism in all situations, and it did not matter whether he was engaged in the actual act itself or just a voyeur! Monica went, and she asked Raven, saying, "Rav, just watch us. Don't turn over or leave. Please just watch him as he goes deep inside of me?"

Raven thought to herself for a moment, *Well, I know she is to come to the Scotsman with me, and we were supposed to go last night but did not. Plus, there are going to be some wild things that take place there, I am sure.* She then turned back, looking at Monica and Chris, then said, "Sure, why not. You guys do look all right, I guess."

Monica gave Rav that sexy smile smirk she does so often. Then she and Chris proceeded with their sexisode up against the window to remind you. He penetrated her deep and lifting up, her hips thrusting her as her back was against the window. She started screaming, saying, "I'm going to cum. I am going to cum so hard."

LDHC pulled back as he came as well, and Monica was squirting damn near across the bedroom of the hotel. It was fucking amazing, a projectile squirt.

Raven started clapping, saying, "Bravo, guys, bravfuckingo." She then turned over, saying, "Make sure you clean up your squirt, Monica, and thank you for the squirt fest. I am going back to sleep since I was so rudely woken up." Monica chuckled as she was smiling from ear to ear from her enlightenment.

That evening came rather quickly, and Raven and Monica had plans to meet up with the Scotsman. He sent a car to retrieve the two of them, bringing them to his place. He had cooked a delicious meal, swordfish and grains with vegetables. It was absolutely delicious too. They all drank. They all laughed. For dessert, they indulged in this very old bottle of Scotch that had a sweet liquor flavor to it. They sipped that while they ate a very tasty dessert called clootie boiled dumpling, some sort of dessert pudding.

Raven knew about the clooties because the Scotsman previously told her about them. So much fun they were having.

Then the Scotsman excused himself to the bedroom, where he later asked the girls to come in and join him. Monica's eyes got wide like a dear caught in headlights. Reluctantly so, she did oblige, following behind Raven to the bedroom. When they entered, they saw him sprawled out on the bed, naked, with a huge dildo, Big Black in his hands.

Monica swallowed so loudly. It sounded as if she had belched. She thought, *This man not only owns an abnormally large dildo, but he has also named it.* He started rubbing it on Raven as she neared closer to him. Then told her, "You know what to do." She started removing her clothing, actually just her skirt. She was wearing nothing but thigh-high stockings underneath.

She just looked over at Monica and said, "Get undressed, Monica. You will enjoy this sexisode."

She kind of winced at Raven while slowly removing her clothes as well. The Scotsman wrapped the belt part of Big Black around Raven's waist. He then pulled Monica close to him and started kissing her, which she seemed to enjoy. Then he pushed the girls close face-to-face as he told them to kiss and kiss passionately like he was kissing Monica. They did as he directed, and it was hot. He then got between them, facing Monica, sucking on her tits while pulling Raven closer behind him so she could enter his ass with Big Black. She sure did put it right up in there. He told her to sit on the bed as he sat on it, riding it. Monica's eyes lit up like bright lights in the big city. He then looked over at Monica and said, "Would you like to try?"

She immediately said, "Hell no. You are not fucking me with that thing. It was just in your ass, and I don't do dildos."

He laughed and said, "Honey, I was meaning, do you want to try to fuck me with it?"

Monica was like, "Oh, I get it."

Raven took it off, swinging it in front of Monica. Monica snatched mid out of Raven's hand so quickly and strap up with it like a pro.

There was a long body mirror in the room. Monica stood in front of it, swinging the dildo dick back and forth while singing, "I got a big dick. I got a big dick."

Raven said, "Monica, please shut the fuck up, and thank you."

The Scotsman pulled her back over by the bed, sitting her on it actually. Then he sat on Big Black, thinking he was taking it like a champ. Monica started really liking it and began fucking the shit out the Scotsman so rough and hard. He squealed a few times, stroking his dick as she was fucking him. He then came very, very hard, shooting all on the floor. As he got up off of it, he then said, "Oh, honey, I think you ripped my ass."

Monica was like, "Well, you wanted it."

The Scotsman went to the restroom and said he was taking a shower and to both come in naked in about fifteen minutes. They both were like fine.

He asked out, and Monica started smiling from ear to ear and laughing like she just struck gold.

Raven was like, "Monica, calm down and be quiet. He can hear you."

Monica just didn't care and was singing her song again of "I Got a Big Dick." Raven just rolled her eyes and shook her head. Monica then said, "Rave, why did you not tell me this is why he wanted me here with you tonight?"

Her response was "I really did not think you could handle it because it gets weirder every time."

"This isn't weird, Rave. This is fucking amazing. I just fucked a guy in his ass very hard and rough with a huge dildo that he took like a fucking pro. Raven, this shit just does not happen every day, any day."

Then they heard the Scotsman say, "Girls, come here."

They proceeded to walk down the hall to the bathroom, where he had opened the door up, and he was lying in the tub. He then told them to come into the tub with him, which was Jacuzzi-sized. That is when they both looked at each other and said at once, "But there is no water in it."

He said again, "Come into the tub," then said, "Straddle me while standing." They both did as he asked, a little confused. He then told them to face each other and stare at each other in the eyes while they pee on him.

Monica and Raven shrugged their shoulders and were like, okay, cool. They held hands even as they pissed all over him as he was jerking his cock again. He moaned and all, "Yes, yes, it's so warm and a lot of pressure from you girls' pee. I love it."

Then he came hard and a lot. He got up, put the shower on, and washed the girls well then himself. They all got out of the tub, dried off, and headed back to the bedroom. He was like, "Girls, come lie in bed with me." They did each one on the side of him as they all were off to sleep.

Morning came fast. It seemed like. The girls jumped up quickly, knowing they had to go. Work called, and they were to drive back home.

The Scotsman was still sleeping because he did literally have the shit fucked out of him.

The girls got dressed, and Monica kissed him on his head, saying, "Thanx for the tongues and thumbs, Scotsman. It was a fucking pleasure."

CHAPTER 19

TONGUES AND THUMBS

Tongues and thumbs could be a lot of fun when you have willing participants. Raven even understood this after the perils she endured, which seemed to be happening by one or two degrees of separation. Anyhow, these tongues and thumbs were a saying to them that they got from their homosexual friend Matty in particular. It was really referring to anal man on man. They said, "Why not equate it to man on a woman or even woman on woman, like when a female wears a strap on." They always laughed about it and found it quite wild, even more so when Raven and Monica engaged in their Scotsman sexisode until one of their closest friends, Matty, was brutally assaulted.

Matty had been beaten beyond recognition. His ribs were broken. The anal cavity ripped up to his tailbone. He was assaulted by two men that claimed to be homophobic, but yet when they penetrated him, they used their disgusting own dirty ass penises. The only bright side of that is hopefully, there will be a trace of something for identifying purposes.

Matty was out one night at the Hub Club, which was an after-hours venue hidden downtown. One would only know about it from word of mouth or having gone there before. It was well hidden off of the strip. Upon walking up through the tunnel to the door, it looked like a shabby dive bar. Once you gained entry and got inside, it was so plush and cleaner than most people's homes. The door was a royal purple and gray with hues of silver tones throughout. There were lush large lounge chairs, and the couches, even the barstools, had an exotic plush look and feel to them. The bartenders were even second to none.

The bathrooms were a lounge room in and of themselves with similar decor. There were deep basins for sinks. You could go bobbing for apples in. Music was always pumping to make you get out on the dance floor and melt into it. As far as the drugs, well, they just flowed through there, so smoothly as easy as getting a bottle of water. To Matty, this was his second home, and he loved the euphoric type of drugs. There were a few times Rav, Monica, and maybe a couple of other girls from the club would go there with Matty and his then-boyfriend Marcos. The M&Ms, they called them. Matty was pretty, about five foot seven thin, a little on the shorter side for a guy, but he was gay and did not give a fuck. Marcos was a broad, stocky meathead-looking one but just as pretty as Matty. They really complimented each other. It was a shame that they had broken up over a threesome love interest that Matty went back for behind Marcos's back. Well, fast-forward, back to the Hub Club, where Monica also would wild out at where she cornered Lucia, who was a hostess at the club the girls danced at, just kissing her, tongue and all. Mind you, both were drunk. It's just Lucia was so taken aback by it. She had just left and said nothing about it to anyone. It had come out because Matty had seen what had happened and called Monica out on it jokingly, mind you. "Monica, oh, sweet Monica, what are we to do with you?" Matty had said.

It was all laughs after, of course. Everyone was "hub clubbing," as it was called, and most of the girls wanted to leave because it was coming up on forty thirty in the morning. Matty, who had his eye on some ginger-looking guy at the bar, said he was going to stay behind, saying, "I think I am going to eat breakfast soon," meaning eating someone's ass. The girls just rolled their eyes, telling him to just come with them and not to stay there alone. Matty, as thickheaded as he was, said, "Please just fuck off. I mean that with the most love, but will you fishes just go? I got this. You know it's like my second home."

"We know," Raven said. "It's just, it's just there has been some crazy—"

Matty said, "Girl, shut up, please. I got this."

Raven often worried about Matty maybe because he was transgender, and she thought people would exude strong racists views of him, well, of her. Matty was formerly Patty, Patricia (Trish) Jacobson, who idolized Christine Jorgensen in a stalkerish way.

As they were leaving, Rav was like, "Be careful, Matty."

They hugged and half kissed one another's cheek, then they parted ways. That is when the ginger-looking guy approached Matty.

"Hmm, you're tight and sweet-looking," he said to Matty.

Matty then swung around with his back to the bar and elbows up on it. Matty was so out there and overly eccentric in his ways, a sweetheart nonetheless that would do anything for you. The guy introduced himself to Matty.

This ginger guy was Patrick, handsome and not so pale as most of the redheaded ones go. He was a good five-foot-ten, had broad shoulders, clean-cut, very well-spoken, and had a great smile. They laughed and joked all up, tossing back shots then going out on the dance floor, grinding up on one another. It was a hot time for Matty and a good release. If only he knew what Patrick had in store for him.

Patrick was a psychopath that would prey on young, good-looking gay boys, jumping then with partners in crime of his and raping them. Unfortunately, his good-looking boy-next-door likeness would allow him to get in close. There was such a strong hatred for them. Perhaps he hated the trans even more. How someone could hold such racism within them was a baffling thing. He would talk them into coming with him to his place, and it worked every time, except for this time. Matty was like, "Why don't you just come to my place?"

Matty's place was literally a hop, skip, and a jump from the Hub Club. That is why he referred to it as his second home. Patrick obliged Matty, and they left the Hub Club together. Patrick told Matty, "I just need to stop at a friend's place a couple of blocks from here to get some belongings I left there."

Matty said, "That's fine. I mean, I want you to be comfortable." By the time they arrived at Patrick's so-called friend's apartment, Matty was wasted. He just kept saying, "I am so dizzy, so dizzy." Patrick held him close to give him false comforting, carried him upstairs to what was an abandoned apartment. By the time Matty slightly realized that something was a little bit off, he was punch in the stomach so hard he vomited. There were three, and one of the three was a woman who held the camera as another guy was beating the shit out of Matty. Then Patrick pulled him close, looking into his beat face and said, "So you want this dick, Matthew? You want it, you got it." He then exposed himself, shoving it in Matty's mouth, not caring if residual vomit, blood, spit got on it. He was saying things like, "Take it, little girl. This is what you want." Then this other guy cut Matty's pants off of him because they were so tight. They then chained him to a brick wall in the apartment and brutally raped him like savages.

As they did, they would give him body shots to this lower back kidney area and choke him at the same time. All the while, you would just hear this female in the background, giggling like at some sort of circus. It was probably a personal attack because a picture of Matty as Patty was left next to him with dried blood on it. This was probably one of the most brutal savage attacks yet.

"Poor Matty. No matter what he did, he did not deserve anything like this," Raven said. He was beaten within two inches of his life and brutally raped. Then he left just right at the corner of the Hub Club, his second home, shortly before dawn. The bar manager that was closing found him and thought he was dead. He was rushed to the hospital. No next of kin could be contacted. Fortunately, the manager knew of Raven and Monica and how they would come in quite often. She just didn't understand where they were for this because everybody was inseparable. Holy General Hospital got in touch with Raven, and she rushed to the hospital with Monica, crying the entire way there. They had him lying on the bed with his backside elevated because he was violated so badly and torn to what the doctor described as a meat grinder took to it. This hit Raven hard and actually gave her a few flashbacks of her incident she thought she had dealt with and had gotten over. I guess you never really do. Perhaps you just find a way to compartmentalize.

In any event, the doctor said that Matty would survive and heal physically with scarring. As far as mentally, that was up for debate. Raven vowed that she would do her best to help Matty deal with this living nightmare, not caring what people thought and said how he brought it upon himself. He just put himself out there in the worst way. When truth be told, it was to the exact contrary of what they say his actions were. No one deserves that hell, that torture. She couldn't even bring the words together to describe such an egregious act. *It is time for some virtue somehow, someway, somewhere*, she thought. *There has got to be something that could be done.*

"Where's the platform for this?" Raven said to Monica. "This story really needs to be told right so there is no injustice." Monica shook her head, not disagreeing.

Raven decided to go downstairs in the hospital to just breathe, perhaps get a coffee or fountain drink. Monica said, "I will walk down with you because I have to leave soon and get ready for work."

Raven said, "Okay, hey, and remember back to when I was talking with all of you about wanting to get out of the game of dancing?"

"To do something else that there is a bigger purpose?" Monica said. "Yes, I remember."

"A political platform could show a lot of the injustices in the city, in the world because, by some degree of separation, there are others who have lived these perils of abuse," Raven announced.

She grabbed her coffee, and as she was turning so excitedly, she said to herself, "That's it, Monica, poli..." spilling coffee and cream on herself, and at the same time, she ran full body on into no other than the dogmatic firestorm, Essence Carver.

CHAPTER 20

ESSENCE CARVER

"Ess, Ess," Raven just couldn't quite get the words out, which has been happening to her a lot lately.

Finally, Monica said, "You're Essence Carver."

"What in the…" Essence began to say.

Monica just looked at Raven with wide eyes, silently mouthing the words, "Oh shit, we are fucked."

Then humbling herself and just putting her head back, taking a deep breath, Raven said, "Oh, I am so sorry. Excuse me for my dumb clumsiness. Ms. Carver, I am such an awkward ass at times." She proceeded to get towels from the drink and snack area in the hospital cafeteria to actually wipe Essence off.

Essence said, "No, no, it's all right. I got it."

Raven just stared at her in awe.

Then Raven said, "But you are Essence Carver. I know you even with that damn baseball hat on your head." Monica then nudged Raven from behind as if to tell her to choose your words carefully. Then Monica extended her hand to Essence, saying, "Ms. Essence Carver, this is Raven, someone who wants to make a change in the world. I am Monica, and it is a pleasure to meet you."

Essence was a lawyer and up-and-coming formidable force in the political world. She did work in Vegas and Los Angeles, California. Essence looked at Raven and said, "Honey, I am just me, doing what I believe in trying to carve my way through to make a difference in as many arenas as possible."

Monica was then like, "You are amazing, and Raven is amazing, and I think you too can discuss some important topics for a change."

She suddenly thought to herself again, *Damn, this woman is strong and humble, not to mention smart and very sexy.* Then Essence looked at her as if she knew what Raven was thinking at the time.

Essence said, "Humble because we are all the same makeup. It is just the different characterizations that define us." Raven was truly wowed.

Raven stepped back and was like, "I was just about to say that, and you just took the words right out of my mouth."

Monica said her goodbyes to them both, leaving them to discuss, I guess, life, the good, bad, and the ugly thereof.

Essence just smiled at Raven—this beautiful and intelligent political force standing before Raven. She was 5'9", very statuesque. She had soft but prominent features, beautiful olive caramel skin with a mystique glare in her eyes. Her dark brown hair was slicked back in a bun. She was wearing a baseball cap and workout clothing.

She looked at Raven and said, "Let's go over here and sit down for a minute. I would like to speak with you."

Raven, being pressed for time, worrying for Matty and wanting to get back upstairs, was like, "So sorry, I can't. I have to go back upstairs. A friend of mine was brutally assaulted in every way possible. He doesn't really have anyone but me, you know."

Essence kind of furled her eyebrows while tilting her head sideways, just looking at Raven very intensely. "Hmm," Essence said.

Raven was then like, "What? I swear it is true. He was really, really hurt."

Essence then grabbed hold of Raven's hand and said, "Shush, just calm down. I now see there is truly a reason why our paths have crossed." They then sat down together, and Raven began to cry. I mean, tears just rolled down her face. Essence was just very stoic, telling her, "Let it out. Just let it all come out."

Raven had eventually stopped crying finally, fully wiping her eyes, looking over at Essence as she just sat there with her legs crossed and arms on each side of the chair with her nails just tapping on the wood surface of the armrests.

Essence looked at Raven, saying, "Do you feel better now? Do you feel like that was a cathartic moment for you?"

There was a sense of indifference that Raven was getting from Essence's voice. Raven kind of tilted her head in confusion then went to get up while apologizing and saying she was wrong at the same time.

Essence then said, "What, what are you apologizing for?" Raven sniffled. "You were crying. Something behooved you to cry out. Now you are apologizing, your friend was brutally attacked, and you cried. Why are you apologizing?"

Raven began to snap, saying, "Yes, yes, I was crying. I started apologizing. I, I don't know what I was even thinking of talking to you because you don't really care. You don't understand shit, lady."

Essence looked at Raven now with a slight smirk on her face. Raven was not in control of her emotions, which was kind of understandable given the circumstances at the moment. Essence knew this. She could tell. Yet she did not break her stance coming out of character, really checking this broken child. Yes, child because she was completely acting like one not being in control of her emotions.

Essence could look at her also, knowing there were some unresolved issues Raven has not yet fully dealt with pertaining to herself.

Then Essence said, "I realize, Raven, this goes deeper than just your friend. This deplorable act against your friend is causing you to face some demons of your own."

She was there before she was once Raven. "Sometimes, things come full circle in life. We must let it fuel us and empower us, humble us. Therefore, we do better," Essence said.

Raven took a deep breath, feeling her rage turn into strength into power. She realized to stop letting the situation dictate your actions. Let your actions dictate the situation.

"Humility is a bridge for empathy," Essence whispered in Raven's ear.

She then gave her a card with her number and office location on it, saying, "Please come to my office tomorrow at 11:30 a.m. It would be in your best interest to be there and be prompt."

Raven, shaking her head bouncingly, obliged, basically saying, "Okay, I will."

Essence said, "All right, I will see you then. Take care, Raven," winking her eye, throwing in the last words. "And no more breakdowns."

Raven headed back up to Matty's room, taking the elevator, thinking to herself, *What in the hell just happened? Why do I wear my emotions on my sleeve for the entire world to view? What the hell is wrong with me?*

She yelled, "You just fucked yourself for sure now, Raven!" She breathed again as the elevator doors opened. A nurse just looked at her as she stepped out of the elevator as if she heard Raven yell. Maybe the nurse realized, "Oh, she's alone in the elevator, strange."

Raven walked down the hall to enter Matty's room and saw that he was sleeping as another nurse approached, telling her, "You're welcome to stay awhile, but we did administer him something for the pain and to sleep, so he may be out for a bit."

Raven whispered, "Okay, thank you, and thank you for taking care of him."

The nurse smiled and walked off. Raven just sat in the chair, looking at Matty with such love and adoration, really feeling a moment of empathy and love. She had started dozing off in the chair beside Matty. She woke up, realizing she had nodded off for three hours and that one of the nurses had put a blanket over her. She started sniffling, not from crying but from the smell of stale coffee and sour milk, which she had spilled on herself four hours ago. "Gross," she said. Needing a shower and her eyes all puffy from crying, she got up, leaned over Matty, and kissed his forehead, saying, "I love you, and I will see you soon. Rest up because we need to fight."

She walked out of the door, alerting the nurses at the nursing station she was leaving and would return as soon as possible. She went home, ran a bath, and got in it—sitting, soaking, thinking, then immersing her entire self under the water, holding her breath with her eyes closed. Then she opened them, staring and coming back up.

She removed herself from the bathwater, drying herself off, just looking in the mirror at her nakedness, repeatedly saying, "I am a woman. I am strong. I will not break, and if I do, it won't be for long."

This was something she chanted every so often to give her strength and to center herself.

She climbed in the bed, opened her upper nightstand, and pulled out a book from when she was little that she had taken everywhere. It was called *Goodnight Moon*, written in 1947 by Margaret Wise Brown.

It brought her a feeling of nostalgic happiness before hell.

The morning came quickly. As it had arrived, Raven awakened to the smell of bacon and coffee and bear claws. She thought to herself but out loud, "Bear claws and coffee, oh, and bacon, what the fuck is going on?"

She entered the kitchen, and Monica was there, cooking up a storm with the cookbook wide open, of course, so one must eat at their own risk.

She saw Raven and was like, "Good morning, dollface. Wakey, wakey, eggs and bacey."

Raven said, "Good morning. What in the hell is all this, Monica?"

Monica said, "It is an important day for you. You have to be well nourished because you are going to meet with Ms. Carver, aren't you?"

Before Raven could even answer, Monica said, "Wait, just hold that thought. I know you're going to say, 'How did you know? I didn't tell you.' Well, I have a confession to make. Yes, I eavesdropped. I played a little. I spied, yah know."

Raven's eyes just widened, looking at Monica then rolling them. Well, none of it mattered now. Raven had to get herself together and get her journal of all the ideas of change and caveats for those pieces of shit out on the streets doing abominable things to women, children, and in Matty's case, even men, that could possibly be brought about if she had the right backing.

She got dressed and pinned her hair up because she wanted to be taken seriously. She poured some coffee in a to-go container, grabbed bear claw, put it in her mouth, held it while opening the door to the apartment, and left. It was like a dance because she did it so gracefully, making Monica smile.

"Good luck, Ra," Monica said as she ran behind her, swinging the door open. Then she thought and said to herself in a soft confusing voice, "Or should I say break a leg?"

Raven walked to Essence's office, realizing it is a beautiful day and that it is about a ten-plus-minute walk, not bad. She was drinking her coffee and eating her bear claw on the way. Looking at it, she then said, "Wow, Monica, this is actually pretty fucking good."

She finished upright as she approached the building seven minutes early. *Not bad*, she thought. She told the assistant that she was there to see Ms. Carver at eleven thirty. The assistant picked up the phone, calling in Essence's office, saying, "Your eleven thirty is here, Ms. Carver."

The assistant then said to Raven, "Right this way, ma'am." As the assistant was escorting Raven to Ms. Carver's office, Raven was looking around at all the accolades she has up on the walls and news articles and such.

Raven walked into the office, extending her hand to Ms. Carver to shake it, and Essence was like, "Please, Raven, I think we are way past that point. You cried your heart out to me for quite a bit last night, so no need for any handshakes now."

She took a filing envelope filled with paperwork and placed it in front of Raven. There was nothing written on the outside of it. Essence said to Raven,

"Please sit. Open it if you like."

Raven looked down at it then up at Essence then back down at it then back at Essence.

She sat back in the chair with her hands folded, nodding her head up, telling Raven to go on. Raven slowly grabbed the folder, opening it slowly. She tilted her head slowly to the side, side-eyeing the contents thereof. Its containments were of Raven, where she had grown up, her parent's names, school. Even the molestation and rape files were in there. Essence saw Raven's chest begin to expand as if she was about to blow.

Essence stopped her and said, "I know you feel as if I have no right, but I do. I am you in so many ways."

Raven started to get angry, saying, "How you are not me and you do not know me."

Essence said, "Please just hear me out for a minute." There was a lot of anger in Raven still. Essence mentioned that to her. Essence told her she wanted her to channel that anger into doing something good. "Work for me with me," Essence said to Raven. "I am very impressed with you, and I feel you need to be with me on my team. I believe we can make a difference. In the back of the folder, you will find an offer letter with a generous salary, conditions of employment, etc."

Raven was like, "Wait, what?" She was strongly confused now and really needed to think of what she was hearing and reading was the truth. This is something that Raven wanted. This is an outlet from the dance world and a platform for her to help—to have one less person suffer as she has or the many she knew have.

Essence said, "Yes, you heard right, and you're reading right."

It seemed as if lights just got a little bit brighter in the office there. Essence said, "If you need some more time, I can give you seventy-two hours to decide. That is it. Then the offer is off the table, and there will not be another."

Raven said, "You have all this info on me because you were vetting me for employment?"

Essence said, "Yes, and for other reasons too."

Raven then looked up at Essence, saying, "Oh yeah, like what?"

"In due time, you will see that it is all good." Then suddenly Essence asked Raven, "Have you read the book *The Bluest Eye*? I just figured since your favorite color is blue."

Raven looked at Essence then said, "Toni Morrison, yes, it is another one I keep in my nightstand drawer." Essence smiled.

At the same time, they both said, "No green was going to spring from our seeds."

Then they both chuckled. Essence said, "Hey, are you hungry? Let's go to lunch. We can further discuss if you'd like."

Raven said, "Sure, why not. Didn't really eat much this morning or anything last night."

They both got up and proceeded to leave the office as Essence told her assistant she would be back heading out for lunch.

As they sat having lunch at a nearby café, chuckling like giddy schoolgirls, they started to become very comfortable with each other. Essence came out, saying to Raven, "You know that I am an openly gay lesbian woman, don't you?"

Raven's eyes kind of widened, trying not to fully look at Essence. Raven said to herself, *Guess I did not know everything about you.*

Essence was like, "That is what it is and another reason why I think many are threatened by me."

Raven then said, "Well, I have read and maybe heard in some circles, I think."

Essence was like, "Oh yeah, what circle might those have been?"

Raven said, "Well, I am sure you know. Doesn't mean anything to me though I try not to judge."

Raven put her head down, thinking, *Damn, I have had an encounter or two myself.*

As they were finishing up lunch, Essence asked, "By the way, how is Matty holding up?"

Raven said, "Actually, I was on my way to see him after my meeting with you."

Really, Essence thought then said, "Please give him my regards if he is awake and let him know this too shall pass."

Raven nodded her head as to say okay and thank you. As they were parting ways, Essence said to Raven, "Please consider my offer. Discuss it with your closest friends if you have to. I don't mind." Then she walked Raven out of the café where they parted ways. Essence went back to her office, and Raven was off to the hospital.

On her way to the hospital, she was playing back everything that has been happening in her head since meeting Ms. Essence Carver. As she hit the corner to enter Matty's room, she saw he was awake and bolted over to him, giving him a hug. He hugged her, almost forgetting his ailments. He could barely talk because his jaw was wired shut from being broken. He acknowledged her with his one eye that was not so swollen shut. Raven could see it, and most of all, feel his pain. It's only been a couple of days, but she swore he was looking better already. She talked to him, telling him it was just a matter of time that he would pull through. She told him about meeting Ms. Essence Carver, the political firestorm. You could see the excitement in him. She said to him, "She knows of your condition and has told me to tell you, this too shall pass."

A tear ran down his cheek, and he exhaled. Raven showed him the offer letter of employment from Essence. His eyes lit up with joy for her making the motion of writing. Raven then got him a pen and paper, and he wrote the following, "If you do not accept her offer of employment, you will be my dumbass sister I never wanted."

Raven read it and was like, "Oh really, still a smart ass, I see. I am glad that wasn't taken from you." It was hard to come to terms with the realization that time had to pass for Matty to heal up as well as possible. She knew that was all she could do for that.

It was just a waiting game. *Life can really fuck you at times*, she thought to herself and thought to herself, *Why when people really haven't meant anyone harm, they get the short end of the stick? Life and the perils we must endure can sometimes be life-threatening. Sometimes, you don't even have to die. There is a part of you that will. It's just facts. The saying that there are a lot of worse things than death hasn't been more so obvious than the present. Drift away and come back to reality really quickly by being slapped in the fucking face going through what Matty was.*

He was a resilient motherfucker. Nurses and doctors alike were even surprised he would fully be awake presently and responsively.

Here comes in the nurse, requesting that Raven had to leave because Matty needed his rest. Raven sighed but agreed, giving Matty her word she would take the position.

"Get some rest, Matty. I love you," Raven said as she kissed his forehead, letting him know she will see him soon.

Raven left Holy General by this time. It was early evening. She went home to find Monica there. Monica let her know that she did go to see Matty early on, and he was knocked out. Monica did not stay long and did not want to wake him.

Monica looked at Raven and said, "Life really is dark sometimes, man, really fucking dark."

Raven then said, "I know, I know, and a change has got to happen some way."

Monica, all excited when she heard that statement, suddenly said, "I almost forgot, so what happened with Essence and all?"

Raven just started explaining how the meeting almost went south. "How so you want to know, Monica?"

Of course, Monica wanted to know. She was a nosy little bitch that had to be all up in everything but meant well. "Ms. Carver plated a flower in front of me as I sat, telling me to open it and take a look." Monica pulled her hand up to her mouth to bite down on her own finger. Raven continued on telling Monica all that was in the file.

Then Monica was looking like, what in the hell?

Raven took a deep breath, saying, "I began to raise my voice and curse her the fuck out, then she stopped me, saying look further because there is a condition of employment for you within there and see the offer letter."

Monica's entire face lit up, but she was shaking at the same time and joy and nervousness combo.

Raven then showed Monica the folder and the offer letter. Monica then yelled, saying, "Raven, holy fucking shit! You did this, Ra, you fucking spoke this true." Raven just stayed, still with no expression. Monica looked at her, then she looked back down at the paperwork, then she looked up at Raven again in a startling stare. She asked, "What is wrong? Please tell me you accepted it."

Raven said, "Well, she asked if I was hungry and said, 'Let us go to the nearby café to eat lunch.'" Monica looked at her like.

Raven then told her she had not accepted it. Monica almost lost it till Raven said, "But she gave me seventy-two hours to make a decision."

Monica then came over to Raven and said, "Look, Ra, I know there has been so much going on, especially with the situation with Matty. I get it." She inhaled then exhaled, continuing on, "The decision is entirely up to you, Raven. I realize this." There was silence, not even breathing, it seemed. Monica then went, "I know you yourself have been through hell, and you're still here for a reason, and that reason I think is to create a platform to get the word out there of abuse, rape, torture, trafficking the living hells on earth we women have dealt with, children, and even Matty, a male."

This was an amazing opportunity for Raven, but I think it kind of frightened her somehow. All was happening so soon, and how did she really manifest with her words?

Raven looked at Monica. "I know, and I am going to take the position, I must." Monica jumped for joy for Raven and hugged her so tight. Raven was like, "I cannot breathe, Monica," barely forcing the words out. By this time, it was becoming late, and they wanted to head to bed, both being so tired from everything that has happened recently.

That night before going to sleep, Raven took out the Toni Morrison novel, *The Bluest Eye.* She read some of it from the beginning because she remembered Essence bringing it up, asking if she had read it. The book addressed the harsh consequences of racism in the United States. She was bold and was strong, not caring what people would think of her read.

It dawned on Raven that is why Essence asked her about the book because Essence is string and bold and does not care what people think of her. Maybe that is what she saw in Raven as well and wanted Raven to own it. "Take whatever weakness you feel you have, and empower yourself from them." Raven realized that things must be told and fully fought against, that oppression comes in many forms. Let this be said that it needs to meet the righteous. She, not even being sure of her own sexuality, knew she was far from living right, but she believed she should be herself and press on.

She said the following as she wrote it down, "I am a woman, and I am strong. I will fight, for the day is long. Whether you view me as wrong or right, I will not cower away from the fight," followed up with an "Amen."

Screaming, running, and sweating so, Raven was trying to run, but it was like her legs were in quicksand holding her at bay. Then hands slowly coming toward her, reaching for her throat. She was gasping for air once they had a firm grasp on her neck, just tightening their grip, lifting her slightly up off of the ground where she stood.

"Raven, Raven, Raven, it's okay. Wake up, Raven. You're safe."

There was the voice of Monica, who had bolted in her room quickly, softly touching her brow and trying to wake her up from this dark world of a nightmare that she would have every so often, each time seeming to get more and more terrifying.

This one she remembered so vividly that once awaken, she could actually still feel the hands on her neck. She didn't cry though. Not one tear there was, just a look of anger on her face with an overtone of strength. She was sweating profusely as a junkie going through rehab, trying to kick a nasty-ass disease.

Monica coddled Raven's head and said, "You don't have to tell me that damn darkness you're going through while sleeping. I am sure I already know. If you want, I can sleep in here with you."

"It's fine, Monica. I am fine. Thank you." She then reached over and grabbed her glass of water, guzzling it down. She switched off the light Monica had turned on. They mouthed the words good night.

Monica left Raven's room and went back to hers, just sitting on the bed and thinking, sitting in a position with her legs up on her chest. She actually fell asleep like that.

It was another day. Morning had come fast. They both knew they had to get to the hospital to check on Matty, to see how he was progressing and find out more about his release. As they were leaving out the door, the phone rang, and they both looked at each other because that phone does not often ring unless...

Monica said, "Just leave it. We got to head over to Matty."

Raven, kind of wincing, said, "I don't know, Monica. Something is off. We should answer," since it seemed as if it would not stop ringing.

Monica answered, saying, "Hello?"

Then there was silence as if she had stopped breathing. She was absolutely expressionless, saying, "Thank you, thank you." She hung up and told Raven the news. "That was the doctor from the hospital calling, saying that Matty has contracted sepsis, and it is causing his organs to shut down." Raven fell back on the wall, exhaling closing her eyes. She said not one word.

Monica continued on and said, "They don't recommend we come up today because they now have him in ICU as he was giving a tracheotomy."

In Raven's head, she was thinking to herself, *Was this the nightmare I was having? What is happening, and why can he not just get better and come home? Maybe he's not supposed to. Maybe he is to die.*

As morbid as the thought was, it gave her some solace, some peace. Sometimes, going dark can be peaceful. At that moment, she felt her phone vibrating in her pocket and retrieved it to look. What do you know a message from Essence, saying, "Time is of the essence, get it?" Raven half smiled but felt a joy she hadn't in a while. She was getting feels for Ms. Carver, it seemed.

She messaged Essence, saying, "I am on my way to your office with the final answer. Be there in fifteen." She told Monica where she was going and further saying that she was indeed taking this position with such confidence, and a smile walked through the front door leaving.

When she finally got to Essence's office. She was downstairs outside, waiting. She went straight in on Raven, saying, "I realize you're scared, worried, sad, confused. I also realize you are strong, confident, and want the best for people you care about and yourself."

Before she could finish up, Raven tried to chime in. Essence was like, "No, don't, please do not say anything yet and let me finish and show you something."

She proceeded to enter the building, taking Raven upstairs to her office and telling her to sit down. She gave her a remote and told her to direct it toward that monitor and press play. Raven did as Essence asked. She sat back in the chair with the high backrest and watched.

She saw what looked like a convention setting in a meeting area or hotel meeting space. It was a very old building from the late 1800s, remodeled a few times with beautiful high ceilings, lovely chandeliers, with golden trimming.

She saw Essence walking around, shaking hands with other contenders and constituents, very dogmatic in her approach. She took a couple of sips of a wine spritzer cocktail that she liked to drink. Raven knew this because it was her go-to when at lunch. She then went to the bathroom, feeling a little hot but not thinking much of it, mostly feeling like she hopes to prove to make a difference, bringing about something good. She was talking to herself in the mirror, crisping up her blazer, blotting the oil residue off of her face.

Walking back out, she said her goodbyes and left the venue. She got in her car to drive herself, which she insisted upon doing. It was kind of strange to Raven because she was a high profile. She was the top attorney/prosecutor at law, which she still practiced while being heavily involved in the political arena. What's next? Running for president? Raven did not doubt it. She knew Essence was a force to be reckoned with. She knew she'd be a formidable contender.

Raven continued watching, turning, looking at Essence, saying, "And why am I watching this, watching you drive now? Weird."

Essence said, "Please just continue. I will explain." So Raven exhaled and continued looking. Then suddenly, the car crashed. Raven said, "Oh my god, what the hell, Essence?"

Six men then entered her vehicle. One grabbed her by the back of her hair, lifting her head up, checking for air. He said, "Yup, still breathing over here. Let's do this."

Then he let her head plopped back down on the steering wheel. Then two of the six men grabbed her out, placing her in the back seat of her vehicle. One other was holding the camera this entire time that he attached to her rearview mirror. They took out a huge hunting knife. Raven gasped. They cut her suit skirt straight down the middle, ripping it opened the rest of the way. They ripped her stockings and panties off, then forcing themselves inside of her one after the other.

These things raped her for what seemed like hours on end. Some of them did more than one time. They opened up her mouth, put their vile dicks in there while videoing it all, making sure the camera never went up further than their torsos.

While one was inside of her, he was squeezing her neck so hard. Then, he'd let go and do it again. He did not realize on the tape his glove was slipping up some, and you could see part of a tattoo. There was a birdlike in shape, maybe wings that mirrored each other. He punched her in the face and stomach if she seemed to move to make sure she had knocked the fuck out. One spoke in a muffled voice, saying, "Don't hit her down there. She may vomit in her sleep all over us, plus we don't want to kill her."

They finally quit. Then they dressed her in her own clothing and placed her back in the driver's seat where she was. They attached a sticky note to the mirror, saying, "Stay in your lane, but don't forget to press play, bitch."

Essence grabbed the remote and clicked the monitor off. She then said, "Do you see now? No one has watched this tape outside of my investigating officer on the case, which will remain anonymous." The air in the office was thick as a badly baked dough. Essence continued on, saying, "This is one of the reasons I want you to work with me, not even for me. This is why I said we are the same. I also know about Matty's condition as it has gotten worse."

"Yes, it has, and I am so worried about him. He's helpless," Raven said.

Essence pretty much assured her he did not have to be. "We must stand up together for all that have been opposed, that have been molested, sexually harassed, raped, abused." She said, "We can be their voices, their advocates because we get it. With the power that I have attained through hard work, I want to use it truly for the greater good. There is no wrong in what we can and will do here."

Raven said, "Essence, you're completely right. I had already made up my mind that I was going to take the position. I didn't need you to show me that shit. Here is the folder with all papers signed and dated. I want this, and I want those nasty ass motherfuckers as well as Matty's and my ex-brother-in-law brought to justice."

Essence smiled. Raven continued on to say, "I want whatever walks around calling himself a man and does shit like this to suffer. Like the children suffer when their uncle or father or priest that they trusted and loved does this nefarious behavior toward them."

Being one of the top prosecutors nationwide that is strongly trying to run for office, Essence realized her enemies would form faster and wider, but it was a change she was ready to take. This strong-willed and charismatic female would not allow herself to be held down. Even after such a brazen attack on her womanhood, she still stood strong and would not cower. That deserved respect in and of itself. She had this. The two joined in forming women's rights groups, enabling women to come forth spreading in groups of empowerment and through understanding. ETU, they were called. Parents would come and just want to talk about how they would get their children back acclimated in just general life with schooling and peers after they were subjected to rape, molestation, or other abuse. Parents that lost children completely would just come and feel a sense of camaraderie. It would help tremendously. They broadened their spectrum to the sex trafficking market where that leaked to two top politicians being exposed and perhaps brought to justice. We could no longer just be the chimps to lions.

CHAPTER 21

LIONS AND CHIMPS

Lions and chimps, both represent something good in their own way. One is formidable and majestic. The other is happy and go lucky, but both can be strong. I feel that lions know their strength, and chimps have to learn it.

A grip on reality is hard sometimes when you're presented with daunting times and tasks. Unfortunately, this is the reality we live in.

There are different levels of occurrences of abuse and abusers in physical and sexual manners—from lower-level street thugs to those that think they're untouchable in the upper echelon of the world. Two, in fact, were Senators Clark Royson and Eva Byrne of Nevada. They are they, and we are we types. The lions that prowl about thinking the other animals weren't anything but just chimps. Time to show them who and what we really were—to stand unified and strong and majestic, to turn the tiles and be the lion.

Royson and Bryne were very well-known senators with very good educations that have an extensive list of sexual allegations from but are not limited to raping while under the influence of sex dens, sex trafficking, and murder. Guess they thought it was fitting since senators represent the state, not the people.

Suffice it to say, much to the surprise of the world, the head honcho was Ms. Eva Byrne, an MBA from Harvard, graduating top of her class. She was originally from Ireland, where she ran for Miss Ireland. Although stunning intellectual, she did not win first place but the runner up. Senator Ms. Eva Byrne's original name was Aoife, some might know as the second wife of King Lir in Irish mythology. Aoife sounded similar to Eva, which so many started calling her when she later came to the US before she had it legally changed. Those that met her said there was undertone darkness with her that stemmed from greed, though she had a way of talking with you that would assuage your feelings or desires to be her way. She always wanted more and by any means necessary.

It was said that she married a man that had young children so she could exploit them sexually.

They were homeschooled and always held their heads down, never looking you in the eye when they were seen, which was not so often, so people didn't give too much of the thought of anything that might have been problematic to seem abusive.

She also helped fund the Catholic church, where a lot of charities were set up to lure children. This was a cloak for her nefarious dealings. Well, some, they thought.

Therefore, Essence and Raven started to do some digging on their own. Raven frequented to strip clubs because she knew that arena and still some of the girls that worked there. Monica also helped out where needed. They wanted to give power to the abused, to the hurt, to those that were viewed as weak for so long, and to stop those from future hurt.

At the club, there was a dancer that was a friend of Kristen, the young woman that was found all clawed up, murdered off the freeway in the desert-beginning area.

Raven knew they were friends. She just didn't ask her name and thought that might be better anyway. Raven took her into the private room. She seemed scared when Raven started asking her questions in regard to girls, young women, and children just being brainwashed and missing, found shot up with heroin, overdosing, and all. She told the dancer, "Just dance and act like you are liking it, please, but I just need to know some things."

As she danced, she looked at Raven then said, "Hey, I remember you. Your name is Raven, right? You refused to use a pseudo, yeah?"

Raven just smiled and kind of nodded her head. Raven then said, "I just need some info on some real crazy shit that has been happening, not just here but linked to several different areas."

The dancer kind of scoffed and shook her head, saying, "All right. I'll help, but I told you nothing, got it?" It turned out, although in the name of a Richard Pattison. It was a fact that Senator Byrne was the proprietor of a shipyard, where she would employ her ex-felon thugs and similar trash to work for her. Knowing these felons were previously convicted of child abuse, child pornography, you name it. Some were ex-pimps. She even named one that forced her into the sex trade with escorting, masking it with working at the club as a dancer. She said that her neighbor next to her sold her own two children for crystal meth to one of Byrne's goons. She was later found dead from a heroin overdose that was laced with something lethal in it. The kids were never found. It's like they fell off the face of the earth, thinking perhaps the children here were exported to another country, causing their disappearance, and both children and young women imported here to American soil via her containers on her ships at her shipyard. It was followed up with her saying, "I am pretty sure they were dosed up as well. Know what I mean."

Raven thought to herself, *Well, of course, children will be willing to follow because they don't really know any better. I mean, if you brandish an ice cream cone in their little faces.* The dancer was frightened but mad because part of her knew the allegations were true. The dancer then said, "So much for the Protect Act of 2003."

Raven said, "Yes, and that much easier when you're in the political arena."

Raven was impressed that the dancer knew of the act, but she was doing what she had to do to pay for law school. Thereby, she respected that.

"There was an escort-gathering party that her the procurers as they were called had us attend. It was well something that you do not say no to. Hell, you don't say yes to. You just go period. That night, in particular, there was a hall leading toward different passageways, bedrooms, and stuff. She said, I saw a woman fitting her description very pretty, looked like a fucking beauty queen, yah know, dressed to the nines as they say, anyway, leaving out the back passageway with two men in black, looking like secret service," the dancer said.

"Thank you very much. Thank you for your time and for even taking a chance to talk to me. Don't worry, this conversation never happened," Raven said.

Raven then left, going home, lying in bed, thinking about all the recent findings she was told by the dancer, and trying to let it digest. The children missing in part being sold by their own mother was a tough pill to swallow.

As she thought and visualized it, a tear ran down the side of her eye. She then sat up and slapped her face hard and said, "Get it and keep it the fuck together, Raven. Don't break now."

Realizing that she was going to hear and see more horror stories as such and if she really wanted justice to not let all that happened to her be done in vain, she had to remain strong and move on this.

There was suddenly a knock on the door, and the voice said, "Hey, Raven, it's Essence. Open up."

She wiped her face and came to the door, opening it. Raven just hugged Essence very tightly while sobbing some. Essence closed the door with one hand. She then asked, "What, Raven, what happened to you?" Grabbing Essence's face, she just kissed her, and they just kissed long and hard at the same time, trying to take one another's clothing off, heading toward Raven's bedroom. Essence had placed Raven back on the bed, kissing her naked beautiful body downward then stuck her face between her legs, inserting her tongue into her pussy slowly but rigid, then French-kissing her clitoris passionately. Raven screamed in ecstasy. Essence put three fingers inside of Raven, and she squirted in Essence's face hard. Essence took her other hand, wiped it off her face, and licked it all off of her hand. Raven went to flip Essence over to return the favor. It was so beautiful, two very sexy women that were hurt and once lost finding pleasure and love in one another. Essence's back arched while lying there, and she moaned as Raven ate her deliciously like a succulent dessert. Then Essence flipped on top and started fucking Raven with her thigh between her legs, grinding and loving on her, kissing till they both came again at the same time hard. Both bodies were quivering, convulsing from the orgasmic rifts.

Not after long, they just lay there and held each other then fell asleep.

Morning came. Raven was up, saw Essence stirring in the bed, and asked her, "Would you like coffee?"

Essence said, "Yes, please!" She then said, "I'm going to jump in the shower, then you're going to tell me what last night was about. Thank you."

Raven said to herself, *Wait, what?*

Essence showered as Raven made coffee. She soon got out, and then Raven said, "Last night was about us and some passionate moments, was it not?"

"No, no, not that," said Essence. "We made love. What I want to know is, did something happen that caused your upset last night? You were crying and all, and your face was a little swollen?"

"Oh yeah, that." Raven took a deep breath and then began to tell Essence the info that she found out and how some of it struck a chord within and made her break a little.

Essence went, "Wait, what did we say, that we'd keep it together no matter what, that we are strong and have to make a difference not only for us but for those that have been subjected to the peril of these abusive fucks out there and for blocking of those that could have possible suffering happen in the future, right?"

Raven shook her head, agreeing. "You're right, Essence. You're right. Lions and chimps, huh."

"Exactly," Essence said.

Raven let Essence listen to the recording of the dancer, telling her all she was told last night. The dancer did not know Raven had recorded it. She just wanted to make sure she had everything verbatim.

After Essence was done listening, she said, "I believe this to be true first off. There are less prosecutorial laws across the Atlantic than here in the US. This needs an aggressive on the ground like approach with this. Although, I am sure there are a lot of officials in foreign lands and here that are and were paid off to turn a blind eye." She then scoffed, saying, "Dressed to the nines, huh?" Raven laughed.

"That's your takeaway?"

"That long ivory trench she would wear, cashmere, I think."

Raven said, "Wait, coat, ivory dressed to the nines?" Essence looked at her bewildered. Raven said, "You know what we got her, Essence. We got her."

Essence raised her eyebrows, looking at Raven while drinking her coffee.

Raven went on to say, "I know her, not know her personally, but I've seen her up close at a friend's wedding, Monica and I crashed."

Essence bounced her head back, rolling her eyes like, "What are you talking about, Raven?"

Raven then said, "I know, baby, I know. There were some wild rides. I will fill you in later."

Here comes Monica walking in the kitchen, "Hey, guys, wasp this morning?"

Essence looked at Monica, just saying hey. Raven went, "Listen, Ess, I remember seeing what looked like a heated discussion between her and Father Vino and her slapping his face also that night. I was startled because why would anyone hit a priest? I was also high, so I did not give too much thought. Then I saw an altar boy run out of the area."

Then Essence said, "Hold up, let us backtrack a moment. You slapped a priest?"

Then Monica said, "No, it was me. He was the reason little Jimmy shot himself. He could not handle what Father ugh did to him. I told you he was a scrum. He's Father Fuckin' Slimo, Father Disgustingno. Now you are to know for sure. You just could not understand and listen to me. That's why my mother pulled my little brother out of the boy's club and camp. We could never prove it, but he touched him. I believe my brother to this day."

Essence said, "My condolences, Monica. I remember my assistant running that story by me."

Right after all that was said, Monica threw some papers down on the table, showing proof that Senator Clarke and Senator Byrne both funded the Catholic churches between here and some in California and were behind the numerous charities under the cloak of the Catholic church, that Father Chaneli was bishop at during their tenure as senators. Also, they were proof of her having ties with the Albanian mob running out of New York. That was some sketchy urban blight, ties with a violent drug kingpin. Albania was the mainstay of organized crime worldwide. Raven said right away, "Damn, Albanian, Vladik, and Jorik. That's why they were so close, an Albanian connection, maybe."

Then Monica added, "Yup, I wouldn't be surprised if my fucked-up ex is involved somehow down the line in this shit."

Essence looked over at Raven then said, "Stop. I know exactly what you're doing. You're overthinking it. They don't mean anything. Vladik was his own guy in his own way regardless if his grandmother was Albanian."

Raven said, "You're right. There are things bigger than me, bigger than us. The world I was in was just the tip of a huge iceberg of evils around us."

Then Essence looked over them, smiling widely, following up that smile with a "dead to rights."

"Bring forth one, and the others will get scared and start to fall like a domino effect. Let's do this and do it right, not from an emotional state of mind," Essence said.

Essence and Raven both rushed to get dressed to head over to Essence's office.

Essence wanted to get everything filed since she was a prosecutor as well and had two friends on the Clarke and Byrne case and knew the judge personally. She believed charges would stick.

She did just that and made the calls she had to make. She then got a phone call from the investigating detective, Jayrel, on her assault case. She went down to the precinct and had to ID a perp. A wonderful turn of events, it was one of the guys that brutally assaulted her. The tattoo on his forearm was, in fact, an eagle, a double-sided eagle. He was part of the Albanian group that Byrne had dealings with. He was tied to the group that imported and exported young girls, children, boys even, and young women.

She didn't get angry. She didn't even cry, and Raven was shocked at how Essence kept it together, remembering her saying, "Let's do this right, not from an emotional standpoint." Now putting a face with a tattoo on the arm of one of the psychopaths that assaulted her, he knew he was got. He gave up Clarke and Byrne, tying in thirteen official Albanian mob members across America alone. One turning point of these major events was Jorik was in cahoots with them as one of the thirteen. He gave specific dates and times of events, even mentioning the fire at the cargo shipyard in California. Raven remembered that story because it happened when she and her friends were out there with one of the containers. They had forty-one women and children, boys and girls, in the container. They were drugged up then exported here to American soil, who died within the container.

They discovered it upon its arrival, and the stench was monstrous. Byrne advised them to torch it so there was no evidence. The youngest was three years old. The oldest was fifty-three. Thusly, they did not discriminate whatever worked for them they took. It was never investigated further because of officials being paid off.

A warrant was finally obtained with the help of the FBI agent Lucas, who was a close friend of Detective Jayrel, and they all went out to the shipyard after being told exactly where the container was and found charred remains of all the forty-one.

Now this seemed to be an open-and-shut case, but there is always something when it gets to this level, Essence thought. The investigating officer, Jayrel, said, "I think there's going to be a senate seat opening up that could possibly have your name written all over it, Ms. Carver. You do good work, and you mean well. You are good all around. We need someone like you, hell, maybe even secretary of Homeland Security, presidential seat."

He just kept rambling on and on until Essence was finally like, "Okay, I get it, Detective, and I so appreciate your kind words. Good to have someone like you in my corner. I just do what feels right because to be a victim and have no one to turn to that cares is very daunting. It can push you to act out in ways not conducive to your life. Well, as you know, I was considering a run for office to make a change, make a difference you know here. For now, I think I will keep practicing law and helping all I can with the ETU Raven and I have put together. We are much needed for that right now children men and women are broken."

Detective Jayrel and Agent Lucas both nodded their heads in understanding with an "Amen at the same time."

A big news briefing took place with having both senators dead to rights and convicted on crimes from sex trafficking, drugs, extortion, rape from Senator Byrne's hand herself of a sixteen-year-old boy with sex toys and forcing him to administer orally. They even got her on child pornography and murder.

Raven said, "I have lived and experienced what some would consider horrors to bring me to this. This is my destiny, my path to give and to help others come to terms with accepting who and what they are to break free from that emotional and mental prison to live. I have found who and what I am, and no man nor woman shall try to define me or harangue me for choices I have made and my sexuality. I am at peace."

"Indeed," Essence followed. "Indeed. There is a silver lining. Sometimes, it is there in plain sight. Other times, it is not. However, this has put a big dent in the sex industry, but it's only a dent. There are so many still preying and waiting every day. They will be stopped somehow, someway because justice will be sought for all, especially our children, the most innocent and vulnerable of them all. They can be broken from such an early age, but remember, breaks can and will mend."

ACKNOWLEDGEMENTS

Annabelle My Annabelle you comforted me when you could in your arms. All while suffering from pain behind your eyes that I could feel and see, yet you still comforted me. I love you and you are missed dearly.

My second father I'd like to say, Maurice Stein I love you and thank you for guidance.

My Daniel Son / Danny Stein, my family, my friend and best boss ever. Thank you for believing in me. I love you.

CJK, we are connected and always will be. We have a bond that can never be broken. I thank you for awakening what was lying dormant inside. Love you.

BC Bissell, you are my rock, my strength, I thank you for everything. I love you inexplicably.

All my other family Susan, Gail, and dear friends, you know who you are near and far let us be strong and steadfast in this life together and the next...Love to you all!

LM, GE, KP, SQ, AF, JJ.

ABOUT THE AUTHOR

Lane is the new author of *Blue Raven* in the book field. Although she has been writing for some time, this would be her first published novel. She is also in the process of writing other books, *Redneckerin's*, *So Do Pretty Girls*, *Irenic Vampyre* and more.

A former FX accredited artist, her interest lies from episodic adventures in women's fiction to horror, where her background of artistry and FX started in which she uses in designing her own book covers and canvas paintings. Artistry in FX will always be something that remains embedded within her. An avid and wonderful painter and candle soap maker in her spare time, she will continue to write and give a story to her readers that touch every facet of the human emotion within ourselves.

Blue Raven will do just that while opening you up to events that are somewhat taboo in this world. She hopes to grow and excel as a novelist that you desire to get enthralled in. She lives and spends her main time in New Orleans, Louisiana, and Los Angeles. This is where she plans to do that, continuing her writing journey to keep you on the edge of your seat wanting more.

Please do enjoy this compelling read from the novelist Lane.

CPSIA information can be obtained
at www.ICGtesting.com
Printed in the USA
BVHW072330060921
616162BV00006B/65